The fury in Cole's eyes made her shake.

"I'm okay," she whispered, wrapping her arms around his waist and hugging him.

"Well, I'm not," he muttered.

Debbie loved holding him. Even if it made him nervous. He was so big and so hard in so many interesting places and—her hands ceased their movement beneath his jacket. She looked up.

"It's my gun."

She yanked her hands back as if she'd just put them on a snake. "Well, I know that," she said. "I just wasn't expecting it. Are you working on this case?"

"Let's just say I have a...vested interest...in seeing that nothing else happens to you, lady."

* * *

"Ms. Sala tugs at our heartstrings with tender persistence, making us ache with joy and wonder."
—*Romantic Times Magazine*

"Sharon Sala is not only a top romance novelist, she is an inspiration for people everywhere who wish to live their dreams."
—John St. Augustine, Power! Talk Radio
WDBC-AM Michigan

Dear Reader,

I am so pleased Silhouette is reissuing *Gentle Persuasion*. This book is the continuing story of the Brownfield family, which I first introduced to you in *Always a Lady*, published last month and available now, as well.

For me, seeing my first five books in print again is a little like coming home. I'm being reunited with characters I created, but characters whom I learned to respect and love.

In this story, Cole Brownfield is a tough, no-nonsense cop until he is reunited with Debbie Randall, the woman who comes to help his father recuperate after a crippling accident. She's audacious and lovable, and she turns the all-male Brownfield household upside down.

Next month, watch for *Sara's Angel*.

Until then, I enjoy hearing from my readers and can be reached at P.O. Box 127, Henryetta, OK, 74437 or c/o eHarlequin.com.

Enjoy the romance,

Sharon Sala

SHARON SALA

GENTLE PERSUASION

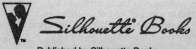

Published by Silhouette Books

America's Publisher of Contemporary Romance

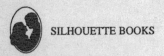

SILHOUETTE BOOKS

ISBN 0-373-48418-6

GENTLE PERSUASION

Copyright © 1993 by Sharon Sala. First published by Meteor Publishing Corporation.

Visit Silhouette at www.eHarlequin.com

Printed in U.S.A.

This book is dedicated to a very special woman who has chosen to share her gift of being a writer with any willing soul who has the perseverance to listen and learn.

Not only has she the skill to write wonderful stories and poetry, but she also has the patience to share her knowledge.

And what makes her teaching better...what sets her apart...is the fact that she does it with love and...*gentle persuasion.*

Ernestine Gravley...this one's for you.

Chapter 1

The doorbell's loud persistent summons pulled Cole Brownfield from the backyard pool. It sent him stomping through the house, leaving a wet trail of drips and footprints in his wake.

"What?" he growled as he yanked open the front door to face a stranger. He knew he was being rude but he'd just gotten home from a three-day stakeout and was bone weary.

He and his partner, Rick Garza, also a member of the Laguna Beach Police Department Narcotics Division, had scrunched themselves in the back seat of a burned-out abandoned vehicle in a less than appealing part of the city. For several hours, they'd watched the constant stream of traffic coming and going from the small, nondescript residence that had tentatively been

identified as a crack house. After last night, that had
been confirmed.

During their stakeout, he'd been crawled on by bugs
and barked at by stray dogs. And sometime during the
night, someone had tossed a sack of garbage into the
yawning openings of the vehicle that had once been
windows. He'd never been so glad to get up and out
of a place in his life. The only thing that had kept him
sane was the thought of diving into the clear, clean,
sparkling waters of his backyard pool. But he'd only
made two laps when the doorbell had interrupted his
relaxation. The quick dip for which he'd yearned before crawling into bed was fast becoming an impossible dream.

Cole continued to drip as he glared over the man's
shoulder to the cab parked on the street.

"Is this the Brownfield residence?" the cab driver
asked.

"Yes," Cole answered. "Who wants to know?"
Being a policeman made him instantly suspicious of
strangers. After the last seventy-two hours, he was in
no mood to play twenty questions with a cab driver.

"My fare," the driver answered, and gestured over
his shoulder with his thumb. "Here's her bags. But
you'll have to help me get her out of the cab. Worst
case of motion sickness I ever saw." He walked to his
vehicle, leaving Cole to follow along behind him.

Her? Cole didn't like the sound of this. But the
driver kept walking. Cole frowned. If he wanted an-

swers, it was obvious that he was going to have to get them for himself.

The warm sunshine had begun to dry the water clinging to his bare chest, but he broke back out in cold sweat when he recognized the passenger plastered to the floorboard of the cab.

"Sweet Lord!"

A familiar head of dark curly hair hung limply over the seat, dangling above the floorboard. "Little Red! What in hell are you doing here?"

Debbie Randall heard the voice. It was one she'd traveled halfway across the country to hear. And if the world would stop swimming backwards, she'd have time to enjoy the fact that the owner of said voice was standing before her nearly naked.

He looked fabulous: all hard brown muscles, wide shoulders, and tapered waist above slim hips. And dripping wet! Her mind boggled at the implications. But as luck would have it, her stomach changed her mind, and she made a dive out the opposite side of the cab and heaved. It was strictly for effect. There wasn't anything left in her stomach to come up.

Cole was beyond speech. He eyed the look of disappearing patience on the cabby's face, reached into his pocket to pay the fare, and realized he didn't have pockets. Muttering beneath his breath, he retrieved Debbie's belongings from the cab, fished a twenty-dollar bill out of her purse, and paid the man.

The cabby drove away, leaving Cole face to face with the reason he'd left Oklahoma in a sweat. She might be a bit green around the gills, but she was still the first woman who'd sent him running for cover.

In all his years as a cop, Cole Brownfield had seen a lot of tragedy and dealt with many situations fraught with danger. But he'd never been as scared as he was now with nothing between him and one slightly bedraggled, dark-eyed witch but a Speedo bathing suit.

"Cole," she whispered, blinking slowly as she held out her hand, "please get me off the street and into bed before I shame us both."

Cole staggered. *My God! She hasn't been here five minutes and she's already trying to get me into—* He pulled his wayward thoughts back into gear as he realized that she was referring to the fact that she was sick as a skunked dog. He took her by the arm.

"Come on, girl," he said gruffly. "We'll talk later. Right now you look like you just flew through hell backwards."

"Don't mention flying, please," she muttered, and staggered gratefully into the house.

"Dad! Why am I the last to ever know anything of importance around here?"

Cole's question came as his brother, Buddy, was trying to maneuver their father back into the house from his latest trip to the doctor's office.

Morgan Brownfield sank into his favorite chair and dropped his cane onto the floor. He grunted, lifting his leg as Cole quickly shoved a hassock beneath the heavy cast. He leaned back and stared at his eldest son's angry impatience.

"Yes, the doctor said I'm healing just fine. Thank you for asking," Morgan drawled. Ignoring the look of guilt sweeping across Cole's face, he asked, "Now what are you so worked up about?"

"That…that girl…from Oklahoma is here. You know! Lily's friend…Debbie something or other." He knew good and well what her name was. But he wasn't about to admit to his family that she'd haunted his dreams for months.

"Oh! Debbie's here! Great! Lily called days ago to tell us she was coming. Lily was going to come herself but her doctor discouraged it. She's into her eighth month of pregnancy and too near delivery for air travel. The only way Case and Debbie could talk her out of coming anyway was for Debbie to promise to come in her stead. I was going to have a pay a live-in to help out until I got back to my feet anyway. I'd rather pay someone I know than have a total stranger living in my house."

Cole grimaced. This meant she wasn't here for a day or two. This sounded like weeks, even months.

"Why didn't I know about this?" he asked, and ran his hand through his dark hair in frustration. Bone straight and in need of a haircut, it fell back perfectly into its state of disarray as his fingers raked across his scalp.

Buddy's answer was short and, as usual, to the

point. "You didn't know it because you're never here."

"Hell!" Cole said succinctly, and glared at his brother, who calmly stared back, knowing that there was nothing Cole could do to argue the point.

"Where is she?" Morgan asked. "I've been looking forward to her visit."

"She's in bed," Cole drawled. "I don't know who's going to take care of whom. I peeled her out of the floor of a cab and dumped her in Lily's old room. She's suffering from motion sickness. You guys are on your own. I've got to get to the P.D." The Laguna Beach Police Department was Cole's second home.

Cole waved his arms in the air, renouncing the issue as out of his hands, and left. Buddy disappeared into his room, leaving Morgan alone. Silence was a rare occurrence in the Brownfield house, and Morgan relished the opportunity to lean back and close his eyes.

His wife had died years ago, leaving him alone with five children to raise. Lily, his only daughter, was the only one who'd moved out of the house. She and her husband, Case Longren, lived on a ranch outside of Clinton, Oklahoma, and were about to present him with his first grandchild. The way things looked, it might also be his only one.

Cole, a detective with the Laguna Beach Police Department, was a loner. Buddy, his middle son, was a virtual genius and loved only one thing: his computers.

The youngest were the twins, J.D. and Dusty, actors who, at the present time, were away on location of the latest film on which they were working.

Morgan opened his eyes, glanced down at his watch, and reached for the remote control of his television. It was almost time for *Wheel of Fortune*. He decided to let Debbie wear off the traces of travel. Tomorrow was soon enough for a welcome.

Debbie rolled over on her back, stared blankly up at an unfamiliar ceiling, then down at herself, and wondered where she was and why she'd just spent the night in her clothes. Suddenly, the memory of yesterday came rushing back along with a sick feeling that the man she'd most wanted to impress had all but poured her into bed. *At least I'm still alive,* she thought. So much for great first impressions.

She rolled out of bed, standing for a moment just to assure herself that the world had finally stopped spinning, and then sighed with relief. Things felt pretty close to normal and that was good enough for her. She pulled her suitcases onto the bed and began to unpack, taking time as she worked to appreciate the very feminine wallpaper and the soft pastel colors on the bed and matching curtains. Framed pictures on the wall indicated she was in Lily's old room. It made this trip just the least bit less uncomfortable, knowing that she was in the room in which her good friend had grown up.

Volunteering to come had been one thing. Giving

up her job as a cashier in a grocery store wasn't exactly giving up a life-long career. Now that her brother, Douglas, was finally out of college and more or less on his own, she could think about herself. Knowing that she was going to live in the same house with the first man she'd met in years who had even made her think of lasting relationships had been another altogether.

But the memory of a tall, quiet man's dark eyes and solemn face had been powerful persuasion. The attraction present between them at their first meeting was as fresh as if it had only been yesterday. A neighborhood cookout to introduce Lily's family to Oklahoma had turned into a contest between Debbie and Cole as to who could ignore whom the most effectively.

But it hadn't worked. It was hard to ignore a need to be held. It was impossible to ignore each other. Cole Brownfield had been a man to remember. And she had…for months. Now she was here. It was time for action.

A quick shower and a fresh change of clothing sent her in search of her hosts. She entered the kitchen to find Morgan hobbling from cabinet to table and back again, obviously trying to assemble a breakfast for himself. Debbie's mouth formed a silent *O* as she took a good look at the mess in the kitchen. Chaos reigned.

"Need a little help?" she asked, and returned the smile of welcome that Morgan Brownfield sent her way.

"Debbie! You'll never know how glad I am to see you," Morgan said, "and how much I appreciate you giving up your time to come out and help."

"Oh, I think I can," she answered, as she gave him a quick hug of welcome. "The question is, where do I start first?"

"With breakfast," Morgan commanded. "There may not be order in the house, but there's food. I have Cole to thank for that."

Debbie flushed at the sound of his name. "And I have him to thank for helping ground me yesterday. I've never been so sick...or embarrassed."

"You're young yet," Morgan teased. "There'll be other times and other days."

Laughter was shared along with a quick but filling breakfast as Debbie was brought up to date on Morgan's progress and on the whereabouts of his offspring, as well.

"You won't have to worry about J.D. and Dusty," he said. "They're off on location, playacting again. Bit parts in some low-budget movie," he grinned. "But they're happy and that's what counts."

He pointed toward a closed doorway just off the kitchen. "Buddy's in there. At least I think he is. That's where I saw him last. And, as you probably have guessed, Cole is on duty. His hours are unpredictable, but he's not. He's my responsible son. Sometimes too much so. But my wife's death left all of us with burdens. Cole took it upon himself to become the father figure to Lily and the boys while I was at work.''

Morgan sighed and rubbed his forehead. ''I don't know what I would have done without him. For that matter, I still don't.''

''I understand,'' Debbie said. ''My folks have been gone for several years now. Dad died of cancer and Mom two years later in an accident. I was nineteen when Mom died. It left me with a seventeen-year-old brother who was nursing a chip on his shoulder. It took me six years to reclaim him and another two to get him out of school. He graduated last year from Oklahoma University with a marketing degree.''

''And where did that leave you?'' Morgan asked softly. There was a lot of giving in Debbie's story, but not much about what she'd had to give up.

''Free to come take care of you,'' she answered. ''And that's what I'm about to do. Where do you want me to start?''

Morgan shrugged. ''Well, I certainly appreciate it, and don't think I don't know what an effort this was on your part. And, as for monetary arrangements, I've opened an account for you at my bank. Your pay will be deposited twice a month. Here are some counter checks until yours come back from the printer.''

''I didn't intend for this to be so…businesslike,'' Debbie said. The mention of money made her blush. ''It's not like I had a job I couldn't bear to leave. Grocery checker isn't exactly high on a high school counselor's list of career opportunities. I can have the job back as soon as I return. My boss already said so. I was simply looking at this as a…vacation. I've never been to California.''

He smiled crookedly, reminding her of Cole. Just the thought of him made her lose her concentration. And then Morgan continued.

''As for where to start…look around. It's all a mess, and I don't think this will feel like a vacation. Believe me, you'll earn every penny of it. If you hadn't come, I would have had to hire extra help until I'm well. That wreck on the freeway broke more than my leg. I can't seem to recoup my enthusiasm for anything.'' He hugged her gently. ''I'd a lot rather it be you here than some stranger.''

She smiled.

He continued. ''And I may have to send you out to buy a whole new set of dishes. I can't seem to find half of them. Glasses are scarce, too.''

''Hmm,'' Debbie mused. ''Well, I'll tell you what! Why don't you go out to the fabulous lounge chair by the pool. Take the morning paper with you. I'll be out later with something cool for you to drink. That'll give me time to sort through all this without disturbing your rest.''

He readily agreed and disappeared outside, leaving Debbie to set a routine in motion as she began to put the household back to rights. A shadow passing across a doorway nearly an hour later made her look up to see that the Brownfield hermit had finally come up for air.

"Hey, mister!" she called from the living room as she saw Buddy carrying a plate of cookies in one hand and a glass of iced-down soda in the other. "You better say hello to me. Long time no see."

"Uh…Debbie!" Buddy gulped and grinned around a mouthful of cookie. "Yeah! I'd forgotten you were coming. Great to see you again, too."

She gave him a hug and resisted the urge to sit him down and comb his hair. It looked as if he'd slept standing on his head. Little swirls and spikes of shaggy brown hair went every which way.

"You, too, Buddy," she replied. "Are you still into computers?"

"Cole is gone, you know," he answered in Buddy-like fashion. His mind was always on an entirely different subject than the one in discussion.

"I know, darling," she said softly, and patted him on the arm as he disappeared into his room with his snack. As she watched him walk away, a thought occurred to her. If she was right, she just may have saved Morgan the price of a set of crockery.

"Oh Buddy." She called aloud through the closed door. "I meant to tell you. You have fifteen minutes to retrieve every piece of crockery and glassware residing in your room, or I'm coming in with a bucket of soap and water and a vacuum."

The door flew back instantly. Buddy stood mouth agape, half-eaten cookie hanging from his mouth as he gasped. "No…never…in here. Wait! I'll do…you can't… I'll only take—"

Debbie waited. He stuffed the cookie into his mouth and pivoted as neatly as a star running back. She smiled to herself. Pay dirt! She wisely refrained from making another remark as Buddy made his first of five trips to the kitchen. She opened the dishwasher and pointed. He blinked, chewed, gulped, and swallowed the last of his cookie.

"Who, me?" he asked, and then stopped at the expression on her face. "Oh! Sure thing."

Debbie left him to his task as she went outside to check on Morgan. A quick glance told her that he was still dozing. She quietly scooted the patio table over so that its umbrella would give him some shade and went back into the house just as the phone began to ring.

"Brownfield residence," she answered. The deep masculine voice at the other end made her tilt. She leaned against the wall for support and tried to focus. It was the same feeling she'd had when the plane had taken off yesterday, leaving her stomach somewhere over the red earth of Oklahoma.

"Feeling better?" Cole asked, secretly glad that it had been she who'd answered. This way he didn't have to ask anyone else how she was feeling and reveal the true reason why he'd called.

"Much," she said. "And Cole..." her voice trailed off into a little silence.

"What?"

"Thanks," she said.

"For what?" he asked gruffly.

"You know what," Debbie said. "For the rescue. For putting me into bed. For taking off my shoes. For bringing my bags—"

"Oh that," he said, interrupting her recital. "Well, Little Red, that's my job. I'm a cop. Cops to the rescue and all that."

Little Red! It had been months since she'd heard that teasing nickname. It was a play on words. Oklahoma University's football team was affectionately known as Big Red, and she'd been a small but staunch fan; thus the name, "Little Red."

She closed her eyes, swallowed sharply, and pulled herself together.

"Yes, well, I'll have to take your word on that cop business. Yesterday I didn't see a badge on you anywhere. Course I wasn't seeing so good. But from where I was crawling, I saw a whole lot of bare skin. Wet, too. But, no badge. Definitely no—"

"You haven't changed a bit, have you, girl?" he muttered, thankful that she couldn't see the spots of heat that had just flashed across his cheeks. *Damned woman,* he thought. *Men aren't supposed to blush.*

"Guilty as charged, officer," she said. "So what's my fine?"

His swiftly indrawn breath was audible, but Cole refrained from answering. He couldn't tell her what had just come to mind. People got arrested here for less. "Just take care of my family for me," he said. "I'll be home sometime tomorrow and help you work out a schedule. Do you need anything now?"

Cole knew the minute he'd asked that she was toying with the idea of an X-rated answer. He held his breath.

"It can wait," Debbie finally replied.

"See you later," he replied, and disconnected before he came unglued. That woman made him nervous as hell. But it was nothing new. He'd been living with the feeling ever since the day they'd met.

"Dammit, Dad," Cole muttered. "You have to help me. Your leg won't heal right if you don't do these exercises, and you aren't even trying. You're letting me do all the work."

Debbie walked into the living room just in time to hear Cole's remark. She quickly took in the sight of Morgan flat on his back on the floor, the removable cast momentarily off his leg, and Cole kneeling at his feet, trying to coerce him into completing his exercises.

"I don't care what you and those doctors say," Morgan growled. "My leg hurts too much to do this stuff."

"I'm sure it does," Cole answered, trying to maintain his self-control, "but it'll hurt a lot worse and a lot longer if you heal with a limp, and you know it."

Morgan's glare met Cole's frustration. It was time for some gentle persuasion. That's when Debbie stepped in.

"Cole, you're wanted on the phone." She touched him on the arm.

He jumped. He hadn't even heard her approach, let alone the ringing of a phone. "Thanks," he said shortly, refusing to meet her eyes as he lowered his father's leg back onto the floor and went to answer the call.

"I'll bet all this exercise stuff hurts a lot," Debbie remarked as she knelt down at the place he'd just vacated.

Morgan nodded. At last! Someone who understood.

"I'd really hate it if I had to wear this hot old cast day in and day out, too."

Morgan was hooked and didn't even know it. Cole walked back into the room just in time to hear Debbie commiserating with her father. He started to object, thinking that she was about to undo all the good it had taken him days to effect when her next soft remark caught his attention, and he smiled. She was working his father like a pro.

"Here you are stuck in this house during the most gorgeous part of the year and can't even take advantage of that great pool you have outside."

Morgan grimaced, nodding as Debbie's sympathy touched his wounded ego. He didn't even see it coming when she remarked, "You know what? I think I'll just call up that doctor of yours and give him a piece of my mind. Why doesn't he let you do your exercises in the water, Morgan? They would be just as effective, and you'd be much more comfortable."

Cole sighed. All his methods for trying to get his father to do his exercises—all his pleading, all his bullying, all his love—had failed. But Debbie had Morgan all but begging to do them, if he could only get into the pool. Thank God for small favors that came wrapped in enticing packages like Debbie Randall.

"What would you like me to do, Morgan? Want me to call that doctor and persuade him to our way of thinking, or do you want to continue working with Cole?"

"His name and number are on the pad by the phone in the kitchen," Morgan said, waving his arm. "By George, you're right! That pool would be just the thing."

Debbie hid a smile of satisfaction as she patted him on the leg and arose.

"You're dangerous," Cole muttered as Debbie walked past him toward the kitchen.

"Yes," she answered calmly as she passed him by without looking up, "and don't you forget it."

"Kick, Morgan, kick!" Debbie urged, and ignored his grumble. She braced herself against the side of the pool, legs astride, and let all of Morgan's weight rest against her chest. She held him in a floating position as he continued to work his legs back and forth in the water.

"Just a little bit more. Only one more set of scissor kicks and you're through for the day. Then I'll get your float, and you can have thirty minutes of play and relaxation before we put the cast back on. What do you say?"

"I say you're a menace," Morgan wheezed as he worked his injured leg back and forth in the water. "And you're tougher than Cole."

She laughed as his last kick sent water showering into the air, wetting her already damp curls and plastering her face.

"But I'm a lot prettier, don't you think?"

Cole walked onto the patio and stopped in midstride. The sight of his father and that woman...together...in the pool...made him feel slightly jealous and a whole lot stupid.

The droplets hit her face and arms, beading in the bright, afternoon heat like thousands of tiny diamonds. The churning water teased his sight, giving him momentary glimpses of that damned red excuse for a swimsuit. It was two-piece and covered just enough of her body to remind him that there was more to see.

And then he saw weariness on her face. His father's big body continued to buck and jerk in her arms, and he knew that she was probably worn out. It was time for the second shift to take over.

"Hey, you guys." He dropped his towel onto a lounge chair. "Leave some water for me."

Debbie almost dropped her hold on Morgan and succeeded in dunking herself instead as Cole's voice sent her sanity into a tailspin. She thanked the hot sun overhead for its presence. It was a perfect explanation for the red flush that crept up her neck and cheeks.

He had on that same little-bit-of-nothing suit that he'd been wearing the day she'd arrived. Only this time she wasn't sick as a dog. Instead, she was more than cognizant of the fact that he was mildly devastating and overwhelmingly gorgeous.

Cole slipped into the pool, pushing his way through the wake caused by his father's exertions. He walked up behind Debbie and slid his arm up and around her shoulders, allowing her room to duck while he took over her duties.

"Here, Little Red, duck under. I'll spell you for a while. How many does he have left to do?"

Debbie froze. Her hair was soaked and plastered to the sides of her face and neck. Water beads were hanging on the edges of her eyelashes, partially blinding her, but she could still feel. And the feel of Cole's hard body against her back made her shiver in response. "One more set," she mumbled.

"You're shivering," he said as she ducked beneath his arms. "You've been in the water too long. Crawl out and grab a towel."

For once, Debbie was at a loss for words. There were no smart rejoinders on the tip of her tongue. Only the feel of him pressing against her hips, his long, strong arms wrapping around her. She'd never wanted anything as much in her life as to turn and hug him. And that was just for starters.

Instead, she dutifully crawled out of the pool, grabbed the first beach towel she came to, and wrapped it around her. She sat down on the lounge chair and watched as Cole completed the last of his father's exercises, laughing and teasing as Morgan began to rebuke and complain.

"You're just mad cause I'm not Debbie," Cole teased. "I already know I'm not as pretty, Dad. But I didn't think you noticed, too."

Morgan hushed. He realized he'd just sounded petty and complaining. It wasn't like him and he was instantly sorry.

"I'm sorry," he said. "I know I don't appreciate all you do. All both of you have done. But even if I don't say it, I think it constantly, and don't either of you forget it." To lighten the moment before either of them became embarrassed by his compliments, he added. "Don't forget you promised me strawberry shortcake for dessert tonight."

"I won't forget," Debbie laughed. "Just don't either of you forget to save room for dessert. If I'm going to fix it, you two have to do it justice. I'm going to get dressed. You guys are on your own."

She quickly exited the pool area, leaving Cole to spend some quality time with his father. She knew that they were close and suspected that having her as a guest had put a dint in Cole's comfort zone. Especially since she was in the room next to his. She heard everything from the squeak of his bed frame to the water running in his shower. By the same token, she knew that he heard her, too. It kept them just slightly off balance as they met from day to day.

Cole was nearly always gone before their day began, or else didn't come home at all. Debbie tried not to think about the constant danger he was probably in and knew a moment's regret for the fact that she'd fallen in love with a man who was in law enforcement. But her worry came and went as quickly as it had surfaced. Her problem wasn't in Cole's choice of lifestyle. Her problem was getting Cole to realize that she was necessary in his world.

"Did I hear someone mention dessert?" Buddy asked as Debbie walked into the kitchen.

"By all rights, you shouldn't have a good tooth left in your head." She headed toward her room. "I've never seen someone eat so many sweets in my life. I'd be crawling on the ceiling if I ate as much sugar as you do."

"Cole has been here for an hour," Buddy remarked, changing the subject as usual.

Debbie stopped in her tracks. It made her nervous that she was beginning to understand Buddy's odd conversational habits. What he was telling her, in Buddy fashion, was that Cole had been watching them in the pool for some time before coming outside. That also told her that he was interested.

"You get an extra big serving tonight, my friend." She patted him on the cheek. "You're a man worth cultivating."

Buddy smiled, momentarily connecting with her line of thought and then was off in his own never-never land as he closed the door and shut himself away from the world.

"I'll call you when dinner is ready," Debbie said

as she walked out of the kitchen. "And tonight is going to be special in more ways than dessert. I can just feel it."

Chapter 2

"Who wants more dessert?" Debbie asked, swirling her finger around in her mouth as she licked the last of the whipped cream off the tip. She amended with a grin, "I mean, who besides Buddy wants more shortcake?"

Cole's bare feet tingled and his toes curled against the red-tiled kitchen floor as he watched her off-center smile and the bit of whipped cream still caught at the corner of her lips. She accidentally found the topping with her tongue. He shuddered as he watched it disappear.

"None for me, thanks," Morgan groaned as he pushed himself away from the table. "Everything was delicious, honey." He hobbled into the living room to catch the late-evening news.

Buddy took his second helping in hand and began a none-too-grateful exit. He stumbled over a chair just as he was taking a bite of shortcake. A strawberry plopped out of his bowl and onto the floor.

"Sorry," he mumbled, picked up the berry, looked at it, shrugged and then licked it clean before stuffing it into his mouth.

Cole rolled his eyes and laughed as Debbie spluttered, "For pity's sake, Buddy, you don't have to eat off the floor!"

Buddy grinned and disappeared into his room, chewing with relish.

"He's not only lacking in manners," Cole laughed, "but he's also totally unconcerned with germs. The only virus that panics my brother is a computer virus. He has so many safeguards built into his computer programs that, from time to time, he even locks himself out."

Debbie caught her breath. It was the first time she'd ever seen Cole laugh so freely. It changed the somber expression in his dark eyes to one of devilment and joy. She definitely liked the latter expression more. Then she smiled as Cole turned to gather the rest of the dirty dishes from the dining table. Buddy wasn't the only Brownfield wearing his dessert.

Debbie's hand caught and cupped the side of his face. His eyes narrowed as he warily allowed her the familiarity. She turned him toward her, teasing as her finger swiped at the corner of his mouth.

"You saving this for anything special?" she laughed, waving the bit of whipped cream in his face.

"For you," he said and, without thinking, grabbed her finger and guided it to her lips. *Oh hell,* Cole thought, as he watched her lips purse around her own finger and suck slowly at the stolen sweetness, *why did I just do that?*

"Thank you very much," Debbie said.

Her slow drawl kicked his hormones into gear, but he wisely ignored them as he answered, "You're welcome."

Chagrin enveloped him at the depth of emotion he felt just being around her.

Debbie stared, lost in the confused passion lurking in his eyes. He wanted her. That much she knew. But he hadn't admitted it to himself. She knew that, too. However, wanting wasn't enough for her. She would have love, or nothing at all.

Cole blinked and took a step backward. He had to. If he hadn't, he would have taken far too many steps forward and Deborah Jean Randall would have been in his arms.

"Dammit, Little Red," he whispered, "you should be declared illegal."

Debbie tilted her face, looked him straight in the eyes, and answered softly, "What I'm wondering is what are you going to do about it, Cole Brownfield?"

Cole sucked in his breath. Muscles he didn't even know he had tied themselves into knots. His fingers clenched. He couldn't decide whether to wrap them around her neck or thread them through her hair. She'd pushed him just about as far as he was going to push. He stepped forward.

The phone rang—loudly, repeatedly. He jerked, spun around, and almost yanked it off the wall.

"Hello?"

"Saved by the bell," Debbie whispered as she began clearing up the remnants of their meal.

Cole's eyes narrowed sharply as his partner began a familiar recital. He listened, cataloging the events that Rick was sharing that related to one of their ongoing investigations. He filed it in his memory along with the way Debbie's hips swayed beneath her shorts as she stepped from table to cabinet and back again and the way her breasts tilted upward as she stretched, replacing the salt and pepper shakers and condiments in the upper cabinet shelves. He could tell by the way she was ignoring him that she knew he wasn't ignoring her.

"Can you come pick me up?" Cole asked.

His question definitely got Debbie's attention. She turned around, eyes wide and nervous, a dish towel dangling limply from her fingers as she stared at the serious expression on his face.

"I'll be ready," he said, and hung up.

He looked long and hard at the near panic lurking in Debbie's eyes. It was the single reason he'd sworn to stay unmarried. This fear was something a cop's wife had to live with. It wasn't something he was ready to share.

"I'll be back late," Cole explained. "And, it's just as well. Whatever you thought was about to happen here, girl, didn't. It's not going to either, so you may as well wipe that look off your face."

"What look?" Debbie asked, tilting her chin mutinously.

"That one," Cole said. His guttural growl sent waves of nervous tension dancing up her backbone as he gripped her shoulders and turned her to face a mirror hanging over the dining table.

They stared at each other, silently assessing the reflections of a tall, dark-haired man and the small, curly haired imp at his shoulder.

"I know what I see, Cole Brownfield," Debbie said quietly. "Or are you blind to that, too?"

She left him standing before the mirror to face the devils within himself that he stubbornly refused to acknowledge.

Cole stared, long and hard. He shuddered. "No!" he said. "No!" He headed for his room.

Three a.m. Debbie gasped and jerked upright, rolled over on her side, and stared at the clock by the bed, trying to decide what had yanked her awake. There! She heard it again, only now she was not lost in sleep.

A floorboard creaked in the hall outside her room and sent her flying to the door. She yanked it open and then blinked, trying to adjust her eyes to the light spilling out of the hallway from Cole's partially open door. It reflected on his bare chest as he came down the hall barefoot wearing a pair of blue jeans with the top two buttons enticingly undone. He looked as if he'd just emerged from the pool. Water was still clinging to his body in interesting patterns, and if Debbie'd had to answer, she'd have had to swear he wasn't wearing anything underneath that denim.

"You're home," she said softly and sighed in relief as she leaned against the doorway.

Yellow silk soft and creamy as warm butter hung from her bare shoulders. Tousled curls, dark and tumbling, framed a sleep-softened, heart-shaped face. Her lips were full and parted, devoid of makeup as was the rest of her face. She looked to be somewhere between sixteen and sexy as hell.

Cole sighed. He was too tired and defenseless to ignore what he was feeling.

"Sorry I woke you, girl," he said quietly, and ran his finger down the length of her upturned nose. "Go back to sleep."

"I'm glad you're home," Debbie said.

"I'm damned glad to be here, Little Red. More than you'll ever know."

Memories of the horror of the crime scene he'd just left gnawed at his gut. It was hard to go from the hell on the streets to the heaven of walking into a clean, comfortable, quiet home. But the knowledge that it was always here…waiting…was what kept him coming back sane.

"Is everything…I mean…are you…?" Debbie saw the dull, weary look in his eyes and knew that whatever had pulled him away from home earlier had been serious. She couldn't continue. There were no words to express her concern. And there was no need. She simply slid her arms around his waist and laid her head on his damp chest, hugging him in a nonthreatening, comforting gesture.

Cole's arms wrapped around her with a slow, defeated movement. He groaned softly as he felt silk and Debbie sticking to his body, and buried his face in her tousled topknot.

"You feel good. You smell good. And no matter what I say tomorrow, I'm damned glad you're here Debbie Randall."

His voice was so soft, she almost didn't hear him repeat, "I'm so very glad you're here."

With every ounce of willpower he had and some he had to borrow, he turned her loose and gently pushed her into her room.

"Go to sleep, girl."

Debbie crawled back into her bed, pulled up the covers, and smiled as she buried her face in the pillow. Maybe…just maybe…it was going to be all right, after all.

Cole woke late. Sunrise had already been here and gone as he caught the stripe of yellow high on the wall of his room. It must be nearly noon. Quiet seeped cautiously into his soul. He stretched, sighed, and then stifled a yawn as he realized he had two whole days ahead of him with nothing to do but whatever he wanted.

Quiet! He suddenly realized it was *too* quiet. He rolled out of bed, pulled on a pair of red jogging shorts, gave his face a quick wash, and ran a comb through his hair.

A note hanging behind the Mutant Ninja Turtle magnet on the refrigerator told him why it was so quiet. According to Buddy's sparse shorthand they were: Doctor—Shopping.

Looking around the spotless kitchen he sighed and allowed himself to wallow in something akin to pity. The first time in days that he'd had a chance to have a meal with the family and they were gone. He didn't—wouldn't—admit to himself that the real reason he was feeling sorry for himself was that Debbie was also absent.

A bowl of yellow and white daisies sitting on the windowsill told him she'd been here. The coffee maker was on warm, with the pot half full and his favorite mug sitting beside it, inviting him to partake. He poured and complied.

Like the detective he was, he followed the clues of Debbie's presence from the cabinet where plates, bowls, and glasses rested in orderly fashion to the glass-covered cake stand holding a partially eaten coffee cake waiting for someone to finish it off.

And, like the good cop he was, he did his duty. The coffee cake went from plate to microwave to his mouth, and all the way down. Full and replete, he leaned back, closed his eyes, and listened. The house was just like it'd been before his father got hurt, before Debbie Randall came and turned his world upside down. It was clean, quiet, and lonesome as hell.

"Hey, Cole! We're back!"

Tony Hillerman's latest mystery went flying to the concrete as Cole came up and out of the lounger by the pool. He was inside the house in a heartbeat. His brother's bellow told him something he'd been waiting impatiently to hear. Family, noise, and Debbie had all returned.

Buddy handed Cole a loaded grocery sack, cocking his eyebrow as if to say, you know what to do with this, and exited the kitchen. He returned with another sack of equal size and began unloading the purchases, putting them away in shelves and drawers. Cole set the sack down on the counter and stared. He looked past Buddy to his father, who was talking on the phone to one of his golfing buddies, giving him a play-by-play of his latest trip to the doctor. A sack ripped, Cole looked, grimacing as Buddy tore into a package of cookies and sampled them before transferring them to the cookie jar on the cabinet.

One very new, but important, member of their family was notably absent. Debbie was nowhere in sight.

"Where Debbie?" Cole asked.

Morgan waved his arm and mouthed something Cole couldn't understand.

"Buddy, where's Debbie?"

Buddy thrust his arm down to the bottom of the grocery bag and pulled out a six-pack of yogurt.

"Mmm, peach," he muttered, and rummaged in the drawer for a spoon.

Cole took a deep breath and then counted to three. It didn't do any good.

"Dammit to hell, Robert Allen Brownfield. I asked you a question!"

Buddy raised his eyebrows and licked his spoon. "You don't have to yell," he said calmly and then shrugged. "I guess she's still in the car."

Cole was dumbfounded. What in hell was the matter with his family?

"Car? Why wouldn't she come in when the rest of you did? What's wrong with her? She's not sick again is she?"

His voice rose an octave with each question until, finally, even his father realized there was about to be a brotherly confrontation.

"What's wrong with you two?" Morgan hissed, covering the receiver with his hand.

"Why the hell is Debbie still in the car? You act as if she didn't exist."

Cole threw the accusation out into the sudden silence of the kitchen as anger sent him outside to check. Morgan and Buddy stared at each other, recognized the guilt each was wearing, and quickly followed.

"She's asleep," Morgan called, but it was too late. Cole was already gone.

Everything dire that he could imagine came and

went as Cole hurried to the family station wagon parked beneath the shady carport. His heart knocked against his rib cage as he yanked open the back door and knelt, expecting the worst.

His hand was shaking as he slid it gently across her face, smoothing the tousled jumble of curls away from her eyes. Her forehead was cool, her breathing slow and even. There was no pale, clammy countenance, only a rosy flush across her cheeks and a soft sigh that escaped from between slightly parted lips as Cole's fingers moved a curl out of her eye.

She was only asleep.

"Come here, Little Red," Cole whispered.

He scooted his hand beneath her shoulder and pulled her toward him, resting her weight against his lap until he could slide his other arm beneath her knees. Then he stood, carefully shifted his load until he had her in a firm grip, and walked back toward the house with her weary head bobbing against his bicep.

The breeze teased at her hair as the sun played across her face. Guilt followed every step. The movement didn't even faze her.

My God! She's got to be exhausted to sleep through all this.

He glared at his father and brother, stalked through the door Buddy was holding open, and left them behind.

Morgan watched the look of protective possession playing across his eldest son's face. A smile came and went. *He's finally coming to his senses,* he thought.

Nothing would please him more than to see a relationship develop between those two.

The door to Debbie's room was closed, and rather than take a chance on waking her, Cole chose the only open door down the hall.

His!

He laid her down in the midst of his unmade bed, shifting cover and pillows that he'd abandoned only hours before. The pale-green jumpsuit she was wearing would be wrinkled, but there was nothing he could do about that. The thought of trying to remove it without waking her did cross his mind. But the thought came and went so fast, he knew it was only a notion, not an intent. He unbuckled the straps of her sandals and slipped off her shoes.

The moment Debbie's head touched the pillow, she turned on her side, slid her hand beneath her cheek, and burrowed beneath the loose covers like a little mole.

Cole's smile was as gentle as the touch he left on her cheek. He closed the door and walked away.

"Is she all right?" Morgan asked. "We didn't mean to be thoughtless. She was sleeping so peacefully, it seemed the only kind thing to do." He shrugged, softening his explanation with a smile.

"She's in my bed," Cole said. "She's exhausted. We've been expecting entirely too much of her. Have you looked at her lately?" He fixed Buddy with a pointed stare that sent him scurrying into his computer room without answering. "Hell's fire, she's so damned little, I don't know where she keeps the energy she has, but it's obviously used up. From now on, we give her some space."

"You're right, son," Morgan said. "You're absolutely right!"

Cole nodded, glad that his concern had gotten through to at least one member of this family.

Morgan whacked Cole's back in fatherly fashion. "Tomorrow, she's all yours. You two take the day off. Go to the beach. Maybe you could do some sightseeing. Whatever Debbie wants. If I need anything, I'll shut the power off in the breaker box. That'll get Buddy out of his room. Anyway, the doctor said I'm healing great. The water therapy was a stroke of genius, and I have Debbie to thank for that, don't I? Whatever it takes, show her a good time, okay?"

Cole took a deep breath. He'd asked for it. He couldn't very well accuse everyone of taking advantage of her good nature and then be the one to refuse to alleviate her duties. He nodded. The smile on his father's face changed. It looked suspiciously like a smirk.

But all day? He hoped he survived. It wouldn't pay to forget she was dangerous to his peace of mind.

Hell! Who am I kidding? I have no peace of mind. All he had was a houseguest from Oklahoma with dark eyes, a slow drawl, and a smile that tied his guts in a knot.

* * *

Cole was leaning against the doorway with arms crossed, surveying his bed and its contents. It was the third trip he'd made in as many hours, and he was beginning to worry. By his best calculations, Debbie had been sleeping for the better part of four hours. If she didn't wake soon, he was calling the doctor. Something must be wrong with her.

It took effort, but Debbie maintained her slow, even breathing. She watched Cole with interest. She'd realized some moments before when she'd opened her eyes to find him watching her that he hadn't noticed she was awake. He *was* staring at her, but she could tell he wasn't really *seeing* her. He was lost somewhere in thought, and that was just fine with her. It gave her the opportunity to look back from a very interesting vantage point—his bed.

How she got here was not a question she wanted answered. How she was going to get him to join her would have been much more appropriate to her way of thinking.

He was such an enigma. Debbie was used to men who were more forthright. Men who said what they meant and left you to decide whether you would slap their faces or hug their necks.

The red jogging shorts he was wearing left way too much tan skin showing for her peace of mind. His broad shoulders and flat belly told her that he probably maintained a rigid regimen of physical fitness. And then she remembered his occupation and knew that it was probably not just a choice of lifestyle that kept him in shape. It was also necessity.

"Am I being evicted?"

Her slow drawl made him jump. And then the look in her eyes nearly sent him to join her.

"How long have you been awake?" he growled.

"Long enough," she said softly, and rolled over on her back and stretched.

Cole groaned. Once. Silently. It wouldn't do to let her know that she was getting to him in more ways than lust. His eyes narrowed, his lips firmed as he watched her lithe body coming to life like a cat coming out of a deep sleep. She stretched first her arms and then her legs and then, finally, arched her back and sat up on the side of his bed as if she belonged there. She rubbed her hands across her face, ran her fingers through her hair, and then looked up at him and smiled.

"My word, I'm a mess!" Her clothes weren't just wrinkled, they were a wreck.

"Yes, ma'am, you're that," he said, referring to her presence in his house. She was messing up a whole hell of a lot, and it had nothing to do with laundry.

"Well, thanks for the loan of the bed," Debbie said. "I feel great! I must have needed the nap."

"It wasn't *just* a nap. You've been asleep for nearly four hours. You're worn out, and for the next two days, you're going to take it easy. I've already warned Dad and Buddy, so don't let them coerce you into anything you don't want to do."

Her mouth dropped open, just a little, just once. She quickly regained her composure as she realized he was about to become defensive. He'd obviously revealed more of himself than he'd meant.

"Okay," she agreed, taking the bluff out of the argument he no longer needed.

"Well," he muttered, "just so you know."

"Right, just so I know."

He nodded and started to stuff his hands in his pockets when he realized he didn't have pockets in which to stuff. *Damned shorts. Now what am I going to do with my hands?* He very badly wanted to put them on Debbie.

She leaned over and retrieved her sandals.

Cole couldn't decide whether to walk or run, but either way he had to move. She was coming toward him with a look on her face that he'd seen before. The devils were sparkling in her eyes and tilting the corners of that mouth.

"Look at the wrinkles in my jumpsuit!" And then she grinned and scratched the tip of her fingernail lightly across his bare belly. "You took off my shoes. Why didn't you finish the job?"

"I thought about it," he said quietly.

It wasn't the answer she'd expected him to give. It was one of the few times in her life that Debbie was at a loss for words. A faint blush spread. She looked everywhere and at everything but Cole. But her sense of self-preservation told her she must have the last word.

"Oh! Well, next time, give it more thought."

Cole swallowed.

Debbie hooked her finger on the long zipper at the front of the jumpsuit. She grinned as she walked past him. He followed the sight of her little rear swaying gently as she headed toward her room. He saw her arm move down, heard the rasp of the zipper as it came undone, and walked into his room and slammed the door.

Debbie jumped as the echo reverberated in the hallway and she smiled wider.

"What do you think you're doing?" Cole asked as he walked into the kitchen.

Debbie was pulling a package of frozen chicken breasts from the freezer. "I think I'm going to fix dinner?"

"No, you're not," he said. "Remember what I told you about taking it easy?"

"But—"

"No buts. We'll either eat out or order in. Your choice."

The smile that lit up her face made him forget what the hell he'd been going to say next.

"Really?"

He managed a nod. What in the world had he said to put that look on her face? When he got his answer, he wanted to laugh at the simplicity of it all.

"I would *love* to order in. Rural Oklahoma offers a world of benefits, but one of them is definitely not takeout food. You either go out to eat or cook it your-self. What can I order?"

Cole grinned. "Just about anything you want," he said.

She nearly clapped her hands. "Let me ask Morgan and Buddy what they'd like to—"

"You choose, honey," he said gently, unaware of what he'd called her. "They'll eat anything."

Her eyes lit up, and she made a half circle of the kitchen floor and then stuffed the frozen chicken back in the freezer.

"Could we have Chinese, with all those cute little boxes of different stuff and lots of eggs rolls and even fortune cookies?"

He laughed long and loud. "Hell, yes, you can have Chinese, cute boxes and all. Fortune cookies added."

"Did someone mention cookies?"

Buddy walked into the kitchen. Cole rolled his eyes.

"Your timing, as always, is impeccable, brother."

"Thank you," Buddy said, uncertain what Cole was referring to, but convinced that, for once, Cole was right.

"We're ordering in," Debbie said. "We're having Chinese."

"Cole's mad at us," Buddy told Debbie.

"Not anymore," she said gently, catching the look of guilty regret lurking behind Buddy's glasses. "It's okay."

"I like sweet and sour chicken," he said, as usual, jumping from one subject to another.

"Egg rolls are my favorite," Debbie answered.

Cole sighed, envious of the instant communication his brother and Debbie seemed to have. "I'll call in the order," he said, and headed for the phone.

"I don't know whose idea this was, but it was sheer genius." Morgan speared another shrimp from the box.

"It was Cole's." Debbie dug through the buffet of boxes on the table. "I think these are my favorites." She poked at the moo goo gai pan, the Hunan beef, and the shrimp fried rice with her chopsticks. "But I sure did like this, too." She was eyeing the sweet and sour pork and the chicken and snow peas.

"It'll keep," Cole teased. "Chinese leftovers microwave pretty good."

The smile on her face was worth a week of stake-outs and sleepless nights.

"Great!"

"Your fortune is in your fingers."

All eyes turned to Buddy, who'd broken into his third fortune cookie and was chewing and reading at the same time. And, who, as usual, had thrown the conversation completely out of sync.

He shrugged, and held up the tiny slip of paper that he'd pulled from the cookie. "My fortune," he explained.

"Wow!" Debbie said, her eyes glowing. "It's true! Your fortune *is* in your fingers, Buddy. Computers...right?"

"Let me try one!" She dug through the box holding the crunchy brown half-moons.

She closed her eyes and picked one as if magic were hovering at her fingertips. "I choose this one. It feels right."

"Read it," Morgan urged, getting into the joy of seeing something old and familiar through the eyes of someone new.

Debbie broke open the cookie, pulled out the little strip of paper, and began to read. The smile on her face slipped. Her mouth twisted, and then she looked up at the men around the table, who were obviously waiting for her to share her secret. It was impossible. It was too fresh...and too close to home.

"Oh, it's just like Buddy's," she lied, and stuffed it in her pocket.

"Have another," Morgan urged.

"This one's just fine," she said softly, and jumped up from the table. "Anyone need a refill on drinks?"

Buddy followed her to the refrigerator and together the two of them put fresh ice and tea in everyone's glasses.

But Cole was not deceived. He'd seen the look of shock come and go on her face. He knew damn good and well that something on that little slip of paper had rocked her world.

"Let's go out by the pool," Morgan said. "It's a nice night. Bring our drinks. I'll get the tape player. Maybe some jazz or some easy listening would be appropriate."

"I'm going to my room," Buddy said. "My fortune is in my fingers."

Morgan hobbled off to the den and left Cole and Debbie alone in the kitchen.

He walked toward her.

"I'll just put this stuff in the refrigerator before we go outside," she said quickly, and began closing the tops of the takeout boxes.

Cole slipped up behind her and, before she knew it was happening, had the piece of paper out of her pocket.

"What are you—?"

"Doing my job," he said. "Remember? I'm a detective...and I sense you did not tell the truth about your fortune." His teasing was gentle, but the smile died on his face as he read her fortune.

His heart is in your hands.

"Well, hell," he said shortly.

"Exactly," Debbie answered, took the bit of paper out of his hands, and stuffed it back in her pocket.

"You get the glasses. I'll get the door."

Chapter 3

"Did you pack sun block?"

Debbie dug through her bag and then nodded.

"Do you have sunglasses, something to read, the package of trail mix, the—?"

"I'm ready," Debbie interrupted. "You can't put this off any longer, Cole Brownfield. Take me to the beach, and take me now."

I'd love to take you now, but there are too many witnesses, and I don't think I'm ready for you.

"Get in the car," he ordered. He turned to his father. "Don't expect us until you see us coming. We'll get something to eat before we come home tonight."

Morgan nodded, concealing his glee behind the morning paper. "Have a good time," he said.

"Are you sure you'll be all right?" Debbie asked.

"Don't forget, there's plenty of leftovers, and I think there's still some fruit salad if Buddy didn't—"

"Get her out of here," Morgan ordered, smiling as he turned his cheek up for the kiss she was offering.

"We're already gone," Cole said, and ushered her out the door.

The sun was bright and hot and persistent. The windows in Cole's car were down, at Debbie's request. The air tunneled in one and out the other, whipping their hair and clothes in carefree abandon. Her attention was yanked in all directions by the intriguing unfamiliarity of California. She was constantly asking questions. And the palm trees lining the streets seemed to enchant her.

The closer they got to the beach, the more varied and bohemian the sights became. Debbie could hardly wait.

If she'd been given the task of finding the complete opposite of the area in which she'd grown up, she couldn't have picked a better place. Laguna Beach, California, with its sun and surf and tropical atmosphere, was diametrically opposed to the wide, often dry flatlands of western Oklahoma.

Cole needed a chauffeur. Then he could have ridden the way he wanted, with his eyes on his passenger instead of the roadway.

The rambunctious wind kept plastering her clothes against her body, teasing him with reminders that the wind could touch where he dared not. Her breasts were outlined beneath her soft white blouse, revealing the top of her red swimsuit. Her legs, firm and shapely, dangled from the seat in a half-hearted effort to reach the floorboard. He also knew the bottom portion of that red suit was as snug a fit as the top, and ready to be revealed as soon as her brief black shorts were removed.

She was full of anticipation and questions. And she made him nervous as hell. There was a simmering quality to her personality today that told him he'd better beware.

The Debbie Randall that he'd first met at the Longren Ranch—the one who'd charmed every other member of his family and then ignored his existence, the one who'd lined up five Brownfield men like peas in a pod to assure Lily that her wedding would go off without a hitch, the one that had sent him running in panic from Oklahoma—was back.

He turned off the highway and headed south. Aliso Beach was just ahead. They parked. He grinned as Debbie began grabbing at all the paraphernalia she'd brought along.

"Well, this is it, girl," he said. "We walk from here. Looks like someone besides us decided that this would be a good day to spend at the beach."

Debbie stared. There were cars for miles, gleaming, metallic status symbols as multihued as peacocks, lining the streets and parking area. Just beyond them, she could hear voices and laughter. She grabbed her bag, slid her sunglasses down on her nose, and opened the door, her anticipation mounting as a new adventure was about to begin.

Cole sensed her excitement. It was contagious. He'd gotten a glimpse of her wonderment last night during their impromptu meal. What would today reveal of this charming bit of femininity? And more important, what would be revealed of himself? Each day, it was becoming harder and harder to ignore the fact that Debbie Randall was stuck in his craw. It would take everything he had to insure that she didn't get a toehold on his heart. Cole, male that he was, was blind to the fact that it was already too late. He was long past help.

Vendors lined the boardwalk, hawking their food and souvenirs, their sun block and umbrellas, until Cole thought they'd never make it to the beach. Debbie was entranced by everything and had to see and sample all that was offered. It took them twenty minutes to get from the car to the middle of the vendors' walkway, and during that time, she'd downed a corn dog, a lemonade, and was beginning a frozen yogurt.

"You'll have to wait forever to get in the water," Cole teased.

Debbie shrugged. "It's okay," she said. "We've got all day."

He sighed. That's what worried him.

The people walked in twos and threes and sometimes bunches of eight—families and friends out for a good time and some sun and surf. Long-legged beauties sporting string bikinis and roller blades skated through the crowded throng with skilled precision, announcing their approach by the rumble of wheels on the boardwalk.

Body builders, greasy and brown as a bag full of fries, bulged appropriately whenever anyone was watching, and sometimes just for their own satisfaction.

Skateboards swished and swooped, their lone occupants performing dangerous yet graceful acrobatics, defying the law of gravity, as they came and went through the crowds with unpredictable regularity.

"Clinton, Oklahoma, was never like this," Debbie muttered.

Cole grinned. He knew what she meant. He'd spent just enough time on Case Longren's ranch to get an appreciation of the peace and quiet the people in rural Oklahoma took for granted. It had been something of a culture shock to him when he'd first seen all that wide, open space and all those cows. But by the time he'd left, the culture shock had been reversed, and it had taken him a week to reacclimatize himself to the sounds of sirens day and night and the growing numbers of people with which he had to contend on a day-to-day basis.

A trio of young males came swooping past, wearing cutoff jeans, frayed and frazzled, with white strings dangling to just above their knees, their bare arms and chests gleaming in a rich array from dark chocolate skin to pink and peeling. Their means of locomotion—the latest fad in skating—roller blades.

Debbie was jostled as they passed. She grabbed at her bag as her sunglasses fell to the pavement. Cole caught her just in time, preventing her from following her glasses' descent.

Something about the trio's frenetic movements alerted Cole. He frowned. They were pushing the limits of what constituted beach etiquette. Granted, it was crowded, but they were still plowing their way through the people with no concerns save their own. A young man staggered as the trio rolled past, and a woman yelled a rude obscenity and flashed a following gesture.

"Are you all right?" he asked sharply.

"I'm fine," Debbie said. "It was just an accident." *Wasn't it?* The last of her statement remained unspoken.

She sensed Cole's uneasiness as she picked up her sunglasses and stuffed them in her bag. She took one quick look at his face. He was watching the trio sweep a path through the crowd.

Suddenly, the boy in the middle did a 360-degree turn around an elderly couple and, before her eyes, snatched the huge beach bag off the lady's shoulder.

"Cole!" Debbie gasped, but it was an unnecessary warning. He'd already seen it coming.

"Wait here," he ordered. He turned to a hot dog vendor and yelled, "Call the police!"

The vendor quickly assessed the situation and

grabbed a briefcase from out of a cabinet beneath his stand. A cellular phone appeared in his hands, and he quickly began to dial.

The boy laughed, almost thumbing his nose at the dismay and destruction he left in his wake and gave one last, third-fingered salute to whomever cared to look.

For whatever reason, call it fate, call it bad luck, but the thief's eyes connected with the shocked expression on Debbie's face. For one slow moment in time, everything suspended, movement ceased, motion stopped. There was only Debbie staring into the dark, fathomless eyes of one who'd ceased to care. The connection was unwelcome to both, but it had happened. Debbie shivered, and the moment passed as quickly as it had begun. And then all she could see was Cole running and people screaming as someone called the police.

Cole's first thought as he dashed through the crowd, trying to keep the thief's bare brown backside separated from the other near-nude pedestrians, was that his service revolver was safety locked in the car back in the parking lot. That he was unarmed and chasing a perpetrator gave him second thoughts, but he didn't stop.

The trio was moving fast. Cole knew it was almost beyond hope that he'd ever catch up. He was fast on his feet, but no match for wheels. And the density of the crowd through which he was running hindered him even more. One thing was in his favor; he didn't think they knew they were being followed. He could see them yelling back and forth between themselves, and then he saw the woman's bag drop to the ground.

Hell! he thought. *They've already stripped it!*

Before his eyes, they split and moved in three different directions. Cole muttered a helpless curse as he noticed something else. *They've taken off their skates!* Now they were no longer forced to stay on firm surface to make their getaway. This obviously wasn't their first snatch.

They disappeared into the crowd, leaving Cole to retrieve the only thing he could catch: the woman's bag. He bent down and picked it up, frustrated by the fact that they'd gotten away. The wallet was missing...of course. They were after cash. The rest of the stuff scattered on the street would only have been excess baggage to someone in need of a quick getaway.

He shoved the articles back into the bag and started through the crowd. For the first time since the incident began, he remembered that he'd left Debbie standing in the midst of strangers, witness to a part of his world that he'd learned not to share. He began to trot, anxious and uneasy. She would probably be either mad or frightened or a combination of both. A slow, sick feeling began to grow inside him. *I don't want to lose her.* And then reality surfaced. He couldn't lose something he didn't have.

Cole had been off and running before Debbie registered the fact. She'd had one moment's swift surge of panic, knowing that he was in pursuit of a thief, and then remembered that he did this for a living.

The elderly woman who'd been robbed had fallen to the street, and her husband was kneeling at her side, trying to comfort her.

The crowd of people parted and watched. A few offered help. But Debbie could see that the elderly man was concerned with more than the fact that his wife's bag had just been snatched. Debbie shifted her beach gear to a better position and headed for the couple.

"Are you all right?" she asked as she dropped her bag and beach towels and knelt at the old man's side.

She missed nothing of the woman's pale, clammy complexion. A fluffy white halo of hair framed her features. Heavy slashes of blush traced the high bony structure of her face and enhanced the lack of color beneath. Her thin, knobby knees protruded out from under her culotte skirt. The indigo tracing of aging veins was evident beneath her fragile skin. A tiny trickle of blood was running down her leg. Her matching, tropical floral overblouse that had been knotted loosely at her waist was caught and twisted beneath her arm. Debbie gently rearranged the lady's clothing.

The old man looked up at Debbie, his pale blue eyes wide and watery beneath the fragile, wire-rimmed glasses sliding down his nose.

"Florence has a bad heart."

The statement made Debbie cringe. She stood up,

scanning the crowd for the hot dog vendor who'd whipped out a phone earlier.

"Hey!" she yelled. He looked her way. "I think this lady may need an ambulance."

He nodded and grinned. Out came his briefcase.

"Now, Florence," Debbie said, as she knelt back down. "Do you have medicine with you?"

"It was in her bag," the man said as tears began to run silently down his face.

There was nothing to do but wait for help to arrive and keep the couple calm.

"Help will be here soon, Florence," she said, and patted the little woman's leg. "My name is Deborah Randall. I'm from Oklahoma. Have you ever been there?"

The old man's voice lifted. "I'm Maurice Gold-blum. Florence and I have a son. His name is Murray. He and his family live in Tulsa, Oklahoma. It's a very small world, isn't it?"

And for the first time since the incident, Florence spoke. "He's a lawyer, with a very prestigious firm."

Debbie smiled. The color was slowly but surely coming back into Florence's cheeks, as was the pride in her voice. She patted Florence and looked up, nervously scanning the crowd around them, hoping for a sign of a policeman or an ambulance or even better— Cole. Someone handed Debbie some wet paper towels. She draped one across Florence's forehead. Maurice took another and wiped gently at the blood running down his wife's leg.

* * *

"Let me through!" The authority in his voice, as well as the panic, was evident.

Debbie looked up. Cole! He was back. He was safe. He knelt. Debbie started talking.

"This is Florence and Maurice Goldblum. They have a son named Murray who lives in Tulsa. Imagine that!" Her voice was just the least bit shaky as her eyes spoke what she dared not say. And then she reversed the introduction. "This is Cole Brownfield. He's a policeman."

Cole smiled gently at the look on the elderly couple's faces. They were hanging on Debbie's every word. Once more, she'd used her gentleness to make a bad situation easier. And then her next quiet statement made him take a second look at the old couple.

"She has a bad heart, Cole. Her medicine was in her bag."

The multistriped carryall was still clutched in his hands. He'd almost forgotten it at the relief of finding Debbie. He quickly opened it and began to shuffle through what was left after the thieves had rummaged. He almost missed it. The tiny, round brown cylinder was caught in the soft corner, stuck deep in the careless folds.

"Would this be it?"

"My medicine!" Florence cried. The towel fell off her forehead into her lap as her fingers closed around the vial, grasping at it in shaky relief.

"Here," Cole urged, "let me help." He removed the cap, and handed it to Maurice.

The old gentleman shook out the correct dosage. Florence opened her mouth like a baby bird waiting to be fed and sighed quietly as the tiny pill went under her tongue.

"Thank you." Maurice Goldblum grasped Cole's forearm with trembling hands. "You saved her life."

The sound of a siren broke the silence of the moment, and Cole quickly began to move away the bystanders. An ambulance pulled into the area. Two EMTs jumps out, grabbed their gear and a gurney, and headed toward the people down the beach who'd wadded themselves into a crowd. A police unit pulled up beside the ambulance. Two officers exited the car. It seemed like hours, but it had only been a few minutes since the drama had unfolded. The crowd began to disperse. Professionals had everything well in hand.

Debbie stepped back as emergency services were being rendered and watched as the elderly couple was taken away. She located Cole, who was still talking to the two officers, and knew that everything was under control. There was nothing for her to do but gather their gear and wait until she was retrieved.

"Hey, lady!" the hot dog vendor yelled. "Have a seat. They'll be a while."

She grinned, dragged their stuff toward the vendor's cart, and, before she knew it, was sitting beneath Wally's umbrella, drinking a lemonade, and listening to him talk about the stock market's latest ups and downs.

* * *

Cole had given the officers all the details and learned that this was the twelfth such incident at the beach in less than three weeks. He absently turned around and then faced nothing but milling crowds. Debbie was nowhere in sight! Swift panic surfaced. She was such a stranger…and too trusting.

And then he heard her laugh. He followed the sound. And when he finally saw her, feet propped up on Wally's hot dog cart, sipping a lemonade in the shade and sharing conversation with the owner of the cart, relief made him weak. He didn't know whether to shake her or hug her. He settled for a touch on her shoulder instead.

"Hey, Little Red. I lost you," he teased, letting his grip on her shoulder tell her what he could not.

Debbie jumped up and whirled around, threw her arms around his neck, and hugged him. She'd needed to touch him ever since she'd seen him coming back through the crowd with that serious expression on his face. Until she'd seen him, she'd imagined the worst.

Condensation from the icy drink in her hand dripped down the back of his neck. He could have cared less.

"Sorry," he said, grimacing as he unwound her from around his neck. "This isn't such a great start to our day off, is it?"

"I think it was perfect," Debbie said. "You're a hero."

He blushed and tried to ignore Wally's grin.

"No, I'm not. I chased those punks and still let them get away."

"I'm not talking about those creeps. I'm talking about the fact that if you hadn't chased them, you wouldn't have retrieved Florence's bag, and then she wouldn't have had her medicine. I know the ambulance came soon afterwards. But you might just have made the difference, Cole.''

"Yeah, buddy," Wally chimed in. "Don't consider this gratuity or nothin', but have a lemonade on me."

Cole grinned as the vendor handed him a tall, ice-cold cup of lemonade. He tipped it in a salute and drank, relishing the tart, refreshing liquid as it ran down his throat and into his stomach.

"Thanks—" he looked down at the side of the cart just to check the name "—Wally." He stuffed the empty cup in the trash, and grabbed up their bags. "Now, come on, girl. It's time to get you wet."

It took a while. They had to make a stop at the rest rooms. And he had to rent an umbrella. But when she came out, Debbie was minus white shirt and shorts. Once again, Cole lost his breath at the small, curvaceous body in the tiny red suit, and tried to ignore the rush of lust that wanted to make itself known. *For God's sake,* Cole told himself, *not now, and not here.*

And then finally, they were on the beach.

The sand was endless and warm and in her shoes. Debbie stepped out of the canvas slip-ons, stuffed them in her bag, and squiggled her toes with relish.

Cole grinned. "Feel good?"

"Feels great," Debbie replied. "Can't do this at home. Too many sandburs."

He laughed. "No stickers here, but watch out for trash. I don't want you to cut your foot on a piece of metal or glass. They police the area pretty well, but sometimes things can get buried in the sand."

She nodded. "Where do we put our stuff?"

Cole had already pinpointed a fairly sparse assortment of sunworshipers and pointed Debbie in their direction. "Just walk that direction and when you see a spot big enough to sit down in, grab it, and don't move until I spread out our towels and plant the umbrella."

"You got it." She grinned and almost danced across the beach in her excitement to begin their day.

None too soon, everything was in place. Debbie was fairly bursting with anticipation.

"Just one more thing," Cole said. "Come here, Little Red. Let's get some sun block on you so that you don't burn."

She grinned. "Only if I get to return the favor," she teased and, cocking her eyebrow at him, raked his long, tanned body with a look that made his blood pressure rise.

He looked down in panic, hoping that it was the only thing rising, and then breathed a quiet sigh of relief, praying that he'd just be able to make it into the water before he embarrassed himself.

The sun block went on, swift and smooth, then Cole all but shoved her toward the water. He had no intention of letting her get her hands on him with that lotion. He was tough, but he'd have to be dead not to react to Debbie Randall.

He followed her path to the water, watching the way her hips swayed beneath that scrap of red fabric, and glared at a couple of young men who whistled and teasingly made a halfhearted grab for her ankles. They yanked their hands back as if Cole had slapped them and then grinned and shrugged as he stalked past. This was going to be more difficult than he'd imagined. If he took her to the beach again, she wasn't wearing that damned red bikini. He'd take her shopping himself and see to it that some more of those tender curves were covered.

He was so busy glaring at every male within a hundred yards, he didn't notice that Debbie had stopped. He bumped into her and sent them both staggering. By the time they'd righted themselves, Debbie had not only stopped, she was backing up. He looked down in surprise at the look of shock on her face and caught her midway in flight.

"Honey! What's wrong?"

The tenderness in his voice was unexpected, but Debbie was so dumbstruck, she didn't even hear it. All she could see was water…going on forever and ever. And the waves coming toward her in ruffled abandon. She swallowed and pointed.

"It's so big!"

Cole wrapped his arms around her shoulders and pulled her back against his chest. "It's the ocean, Little Red. It's supposed to be big." And then something occurred to him. "Haven't you ever seen the ocean?"

She shook her head, unable to speak for a moment.

"I've seen ponds. I've seen creeks. I've even seen rivers in flood. But every time, I could see land on the other side, too. I've never seen water and not seen it's boundary."

"Well, you have now," he said. "Deborah Jean, welcome to the Pacific." He scooped her up in his arms, and began walking with her toward the waves lapping at the shoreline.

Her arms tightened around his neck. "Cole?"

"I wouldn't scare you on purpose, and you know it. Calm down. We're just going to meet it together."

The look on his face told her more than he'd meant to tell. She saw trust. She saw strength. And she saw something else Cole Brownfield never knew was showing. She saw tenderness…and desire.

At first the water felt cold. But the sun was hot, and the water refreshed them. Cole held her close against his body and let the waters tease her until Debbie felt comfortable with its rhythm.

"You can put me down now," she said. And then when he began to comply, she cautioned nervously, "Just don't go too far."

Cole grimaced. He was already drowning in those wide, dark eyes. He wasn't going anywhere unless Debbie went with him.

It was late. Debbie was asleep beneath the umbrella's shade as Cole kept watch. And he was desperately watching everything and everyone except the woman lying beside him. He didn't care. He'd already tried it and nearly lost his sanity at the thought of stretching out beside her, slipping her against and then beneath him, and losing himself in—

"Hey, Brownfield! As I live and breathe. I never thought I'd see you down here among the pretty boys and beach bunnies."

Cole looked up and grinned, recognizing the smart-ass tone before he saw its owner.

"Hey, yourself, Whaley. I see you're riding herd today." His remark was pointedly aimed at Detective Lee Whaley's two teenage daughters, who were doing their best to attract any or all male eyes their way.

Lee rolled his eyes and grimaced. "I couldn't have had boys. Hell no. I had to have girls—four to be exact. I'll never survive their raising. I'll probably wind up in the stir for murder first."

Cole laughed. "You love it and you know it. And if you hadn't been such a hell raiser when you were a kid, you would trust these boys more."

Lee grinned. He plopped his short, stocky body down beside Cole, patted his head to make sure his well-worn golf hat was still covering his nearly bald head, and picked at a spot on his arm where skin was trying to peel. He kicked a spray of sand on Cole's feet as a retort. It was then that he saw the curvy little female lying beside and behind him.

"What have we here?" he leered, and elbowed Cole

in return for the glare he was receiving. "Been holding out on us, have you?"

Cole glared again. "She's a houseguest," he said shortly. "She's my sister Lily's friend from Oklahoma. She came to help out with Dad while his leg heals."

The smirk slid off Lee Whaley's face. "How *is* Morgan, anyway? That was a hell of a wreck. He was lucky he wasn't killed."

Cole nodded. "Thanks to her," he tilted his head toward Debbie, unaware that his expression and voice had softened, "he's doing much better. She's got him doing his exercises, and has him on a regular schedule of healthy diet and rest. She could charm roses into growing without thorns."

Lee grinned again. "Well, she's got her work cut out for her. You're still full of thorns, buddy. In fact, you're prickly as hell."

Cole tried to maintain his disparaging attitude, but it was no use. Lee Whaley was too good a friend, and too close to the mark to deny.

"Say," Lee said. "Why don't you two guys come on over later. We're having a clam bake in the backyard. Remember where we live? Just past the beach, first house on your left. It'll be the one with all the boys lined up at my fence, gawking."

Cole laughed.

Whaley took a lot of teasing about his residence. The ribbing ranged from accusations that he took kickbacks to suggestions he was stealing drug money. But it was all in good fun and Whaley knew it. He'd just had the good fortune to marry his high school sweetheart. She'd had the good fortune to be the only child of a wealthy, retired movie mogul. Ten years ago, her parents had died and left her everything, including a very ostentatious beachfront home. Whaley had taken it in his stride. He was a cop. Just because his wife had money didn't mean he was going to give up his own pension. He had too much pride in himself and his work to do that.

And then Debbie's voice startled them both as she crawled to her knees and entwined herself against Cole's back.

"We'd love to, wouldn't we?" she asked, and slid her elbows on either side of Cole's face, resting them on his shoulders.

The feel of those lush breasts pushing against his spine gave him an instant ache he couldn't afford, especially not in front of Whaley. The little devil. He hadn't even known she was awake. He grabbed her arms and wrapped them around his neck.

Lee smiled, watching them fencing with bodies and words. He vaguely remembered what it was like to be so desperately in love and not be able to do anything about it. Thank goodness he had Charlotte. She'd put up with nearly twenty years of him and police work, plus the fact that he'd refused to give it up. She deserved a medal. But she'd settled for him.

Cole was afraid to let go of Debbie's arms. He never knew what she was going to do, and he didn't want any more surprises in front of Lee. "Are you going to have a crowd?"

Lee nodded. "You know how these things get. Just bring yourselves. We'll eat around sunset."

"We'll be there," Cole said.

Lee nodded his approval, then looked up and saw that his daughters were swiftly disappearing down the beach with several young men in tow.

"Oh hell," he muttered. "I've got to go. I promised Charlotte that I'd sort through the uninvited guests this time. Last time, the girls brought home someone who couldn't speak English, but kept flashing a wad of dough that would choke a horse. Those kind make me nervous. Know what I mean?"

Cole grinned and waved goodbye as Lee made his way down the beach, following in his daughters' wake.

"He's nice," Debbie said.

"So are you," Cole answered as he pulled her around and into his lap.

The look he gave her was one that she'd save forever in her memory.

"Thank you very much, Cole."

Her voice was soft and gentle. He ached to taste the words on her lips.

"You're very welcome," he said, and settled for less.

Chapter 4

"Are you cold?"

Cole's voice wrapped around Debbie's senses, making the breath she'd been taking harder to swallow. She scooted closer to the bonfire and turned her back to the flames, giving equal time to her shivering body.

"Just a little. I think it's the breeze coming off the ocean."

"Hold up your arms," Cole asked.

"Are you going to rob me?" she teased as she threaded her arms through the sleeves of the sweatshirt he was pulling over her head.

"I haven't quite decided what to do with you, girl."

His voice was low and steady, nothing like his heart. It rocked against his chest like a boat in a storm.

She smiled and rubbed her hands against the welcome warmth covering her arms.

"The sweatshirt's either J.D.'s or Dusty's." Cole answered her question before it was asked. "It was in my trunk. I found it when I went to get my sweats. Good thing they're a lot shorter than I am, or you'd be lost in here." He ruffled the top of her curls. "I also found the matching pants. Want to try them? They have elastic at the ankles and a drawstring waist."

"Please." Debbie was trying to keep her teeth from chattering.

She used Cole for a leaning post and quickly thrust her legs into the blue sweats. They bagged around her ankles as she tried to find the drawstring at the waist.

"Here, let me," Cole said, and slid his hands beneath the sweat shirt, fumbling in the semidarkness surrounding the bonfire Lee Whaley had built at the edge of his property.

Debbie held her breath, closed her eyes, and pretended that the touch of his hands at her waist was a prelude to more.

The voices of the other guests at the Whaley residence faded into the background as they ranged from the second-story deck of the home to the water's edge and scattered along the beach. People were more than replete from the evening's meal and trying to walk off their binge.

Cole had wanted to do the same, but for different reasons. He'd hardly eaten a thing, for watching Debbie mingling with his friends. The men had begun to reminisce about a narcotics bust they'd made last year that had made national news. The longer they'd talked, the more graphic their stories became. They were too proud of the fact that they'd taken down one of the larger drug lords in the area to let it be forgotten.

Cole sat and waited for a reaction from Debbie that never came.

She listened. Cole started to think she was going to let it slide. But what she finally said wasn't what he'd expected. It wasn't horror at the tales, and it wasn't a put-down of their occupations. She'd simply caught one of the men in a slight fabrication of the truth.

"I don't see how that happened," Debbie said, trying not to grin at a statement one of the men had just made.

"What don't you see, little lady?" the detective asked. He rolled his eyes at Cole, thinking he was going to get her good.

"Well…just a few minutes ago, you said you fainted at the sight of blood. If that's true, then I don't see how you managed to take the entire bunch into custody alone. You said they were 'all shot up.'"

The men erupted into laughter as the off-duty officer grinned at Debbie's remark.

"Yeah, I do," he'd answered. "But I always manage to slap the cuffs on them before I pass out."

Cole had laughed along with them. Instinctively she'd hit on the right note with these guys. They were serious when it mattered and got through the horror of what they saw by laughing at it.

He wanted to believe she could fit in. He wanted to believe that he could begin a life with her. He wanted to, but the certainty wasn't there. Debbie *might* be strong enough...but he didn't know if he was strong enough to lose her if she wasn't.

He tugged at the drawstrings and then tied them snugly, tucking the dangling ends inside the pants.

"That better?"

Debbie nodded and opened her eyes, willing him to make a move. He did.

"Want to go for a walk?" Cole held his breath, waiting for her to answer.

"I thought you'd never ask."

The tide had swallowed the shoreline as Debbie knew it. It was another something that would take getting used to. In Oklahoma, water stayed put. Except for intermittent floods in certain areas, water pretty much knew its place.

The words of an old Gatlin Brothers' song came to mind. She didn't know about all the gold still being in California, but California *definitely* was a brand new game.

Her foot crunched upon something half-buried in the sand. She bent down, dug until she found it, and lifted it up, using the moonlight to see by. It was a shell. Small convoluted swirls formed the white conical shape into something special and secret.

"Look!" she cried. "My first seashell!"

Cole caught her hand and carried it to his lips. "You've had a lot of firsts today, haven't you, lady?"

There was something about the way he was touching her, something in his voice that gave her hope.

"It was my first time to see the ocean." Her voice was breathless and soft. "It was my first time to eat clams." His hands cupped her face and tilted it. "I found my first—"

His mouth took the rest of her words as his hands stole her heart.

It was better than she'd imagined. His lips were cool and firm, softening and warming as she opened to him. His hands made tentative forays across her shoulders, then moved back up her neck and threaded the tangled curls around her face.

He shuddered and groaned as her arms wrapped around his waist and pulled him close...too close...not close enough.

Moonlight sliced a thin, silver path across the water, blinding in its intensity, but neither saw it. They were too lost in the feel of being in each other's arms.

And then suddenly Cole couldn't get close enough. He took them to their knees. His hands moved beneath her shirt and around behind her back.

The catch on her red bikini top came undone, and she spilled into his palms with a thrust, yearning to alleviate the pulsing pressure he'd created.

The soft tips went flat against his hands and then, as if they had a life of their own, hardened and pushed against him, reminding him that he'd started something that was aching to be finished.

With no thought of their proximity to the other

guests, he laid her beneath him, stretched out above her, and then branded himself with her heat. She was soft. All movement and enticing depths that he wanted to explore. She would let him. Of that, he was certain. Could he let himself? Of that, he was unsure.

The sand made a place for her, generously shifting to allow her room—room for her body and the man above her. Below the surface, it was still warm from the heat of the day. Debbie sighed and lifted her arms, pulling Cole down until there was no room for breath between them. She heard his soft groan and felt his need as his mouth plundered past the neckline of the sweat shirt. His hands slid up, and then his hands slid down. And Debbie lifted herself to meet them.

"Jesus!" Whether he'd said it as a prayer or an oath, he was uncertain. But nevertheless, Cole rolled off Debbie and sat up, burying his face in his hands as he desperately tried to regain control of what he'd nearly lost. His sanity.

"My God!" he muttered, remembering that he'd left her behind, and scooped her from the sand. He sandwiched her between his knees, fitting her backside to his lap as he tried to get himself in order. "Debbie...I'm sorry. I didn't mean to—"

"For Pete's sake," she mumbled, as his chin nestled in the curls atop her head, "if you ever expect me to speak to you again, at least don't apologize."

He shuddered, wrapped her tightly in his arms, and wondered if he could ever let her go. He rocked them in the darkness.

The moon's silver path on the water beckoned, enticing by its mere presence, promising something intangible if one were courageous enough to chance it.

Both stared, lost in the lure of the night, and knew that if they were only brave enough to walk on water, magic awaited. But neither moved.

The drive home was long; Debbie, strangely silent. It was so unlike her, Cole was uneasy. He couldn't tell whether he'd angered her by initiating the kiss or by stopping just beyond. Either way, she was quiet and he was nervous.

But tonight, he'd realized something. For the first time in his entire life, he was considering the possibility of ending his life as a bachelor. For the first time, he let himself contemplate what it would be like to share his life with another. It would mean that his peace of mind, his sanity, his well-being would not depend entirely upon himself. It would revolve around another person and her happiness and her well-being and peace of mind. It would mean that Cole was not in control. It scared the hell out of him.

"We're home," Debbie said quietly.

It startled him.

She spoke again. "I'll get the bag. You get the rest of the stuff. Just dump the entire mess in the back room, okay? I'll go through it all tomorrow. I'm too tired to deal with it now."

He parked, opened the door, and started around to help her out. But she beat him to it and let herself out of the car. He sighed with frustration, turned, and headed for the back door, key in hand.

She walked past him, into the shadowy depths of the house, homing in on the hall light shining through the kitchen, guiding the way toward their rooms.

"Debbie?"

His voice caught and held her in place. Finally she turned and answered. He was impossible to ignore. "What?"

"Are you all right?"

She shrugged in the darkness, but he still saw...or sensed the motion. "Of course."

"Then...where are you going in such a hurry? I thought you might want something to drink...maybe unwind..."

"I'm going to take a shower," she said quietly. "I need to wash the sand out of my hair."

It left him speechless. Memories of her beneath him in the sand, and her body soft and inviting, made him instantly hard and aching. She walked away, and he let her.

It was only much later when Debbie lay sleepless, staring out at the moonlight teasing the folds of the curtain at her windows, that she remembered she hadn't told Cole she'd seen the mugger's face.

Morgan sensed something had changed. Ever since their day at the beach, he'd felt the chill between them.

He saw his son's silent anguish. When Debbie came in a room, Cole made an excuse to exit. If she needed something, he was the first to volunteer to get it, but always managed to return and leave it without having to face her. Morgan wanted to shake them both. It would have been obvious to a blind man with earmuffs that they were doing everything but what they wanted…and that was to fall into each other's arms.

Cole had volunteered for a very extended and very dangerous assignment, and Morgan knew it was just an excuse to keep from facing what he was trying to ignore. Debbie. He missed his son, and he worried about him, but except for saying a prayer each night, there was nothing he could do but be there, should they need a sounding board.

Debbie smiled and laughed. She cooked and cleaned. She crawled into the pool and chided and teased Morgan through all his physical therapy. She coerced Buddy into joining them for meals so that she and Morgan wouldn't be alone. There was no way she was going to admit aloud, to anyone, that she and Cole were having problems. She couldn't admit it aloud, because she'd yet to admit it silently, to herself.

He's just stubborn. That was her rationale for everything that made her ache. That was what kept her from packing her bags and taking the next plane back to Oklahoma. That was the only thing that kept her in her own room at night and not across the hall between the covers of his empty bed.

I can be just as stubborn. That was what kept her from falling apart every time she heard a siren. And when she listened to the local evening news, she did not let on, by so much as a gasp, that the latest drug bust had resulted in two deaths.

Learning that the deaths had not been of the officers involved, but of some suspects who'd resisted arrest, did not help. It only served to remind Debbie that during his days on duty, Cole was constantly in the line of fire and in danger of never coming home.

It made her stop. And it made her think. And for the first time, she had a taste of what kept Cole Brownfield out of her arms. She'd heard him say more than once that, on the job, a policeman's first duty was to his partner. It was what got them home safe and sound each day. And that if a man, or woman, as the case might be, couldn't face that fact, they had no business trying to work a family into a policeman's lifestyle. It was what got people killed.

But Debbie knew that she could face sharing Cole. If that was what it took to keep him safe and bring him home, she'd share him with the whole damned department. *I can be stubborn,* she reminded herself. *I will wait until he realizes that, too.*

She sprayed furniture polish on an already gleaming table and rubbed furiously, muttering beneath her breath at the stupidity of supposedly brilliant people.

"Were you talking about me?" Buddy asked as he wandered through the kitchen with an empty plate and glass. He'd long since learned to return his carry-out crockery. It still gave him nightmares thinking about soap and water and vacuums in his inner sanctum.

"What?" Debbie looked up, startled at his appearance and then realized that he'd walked in on the last of her mumblings.

"Brilliant people...were you talking about me?" Buddy grinned.

"You're not nearly as stupid as you let on, are you, Robert Allen?"

"Cole just drove up." He deposited his announcement and his dirty dishes at the same time.

Debbie whirled around, stared through the living room toward the front door and then, before she thought, wrapped her arms around Buddy's neck and planted a big kiss on his cheek.

"Thank you for caring, Buddy dear," she whispered.

Cole walked in. It was the first thing he saw. His brother and Debbie. In the kitchen. Kissing. At least she was kissing, Buddy was grinning down at her like someone had just handed him the keys to the computer brain in Washington, D.C.

Cole didn't think. He just reacted. It had been too long since he'd been home and too long since he'd felt human. He'd never been so pissed off in his life. He pivoted, slamming the door behind him as he made a none-too-graceful exit back outside. This time, he stood on the front stoop, leaned against the door, placed his finger on the bell, and pushed.

Debbie grinned. She'd heard the door open, and then she'd heard it slam. For just a moment, she feared that the impulse she'd given in to with Buddy had been the wrong thing to do. The last thing she meant to cause was trouble between brothers. However, it was obvious from the sarcastic ringing of the doorbell that Cole hadn't mistaken what she'd been doing. He was just mad that it hadn't been him.

"I'm going to my room now," Buddy said. "Thank you for the kiss…and we're out of cookies."

"Okay. You're welcome. And I'll make some tomorrow."

He nodded, secure in the knowledge that he'd done his bit toward family unity.

Morgan hobbled into the room, intent on reaming out whoever was playing at his door, when Debbie made a dash into the living room. He caught a glimpse of Cole's angry face through the sheer curtains, another glimpse of the light shining in her eyes, and did as neat a pivot as his leg would allow.

"I'm going to my room," he announced.

Debbie grinned. "It runs in the family."

He didn't' know what she was talking about, but he kept walking just the same. If it was the last thing he saw on this earth, he wanted to see Cole and Debbie together…and happy.

Debbie took a deep breath and opened the door. Cole's glare was as dark as the three-day growth of beard on his face.

"Hi!" she said. "You need a shave."

She turned and walked away, leaving him standing on the doorstep. She hadn't seen or heard from him in more than seventy-two hours. It was the single hardest thing she'd ever done.

Cole stared. *How in hell do you stay mad at someone who won't fight back?* He walked in, slamming the door behind him, and followed her into the kitchen on the pretext of getting himself something to eat.

Doors banged, dishes rattled, pots and bowls were shifted, and the remnants of the refrigerator received a thorough inspection. He stared and he glared at everything and everywhere...but at Debbie.

"Looks like you've been busy while I've been gone." The remark was meant to be sarcastic. He was referring to walking in on the kiss.

"Yes. Your dad is now down to a cane instead of crutches. I painted the fence around the pool. The neighbor across the street gave me some apricots today. I froze six quart bagfuls. They're really good. Do you like apricots? I could make a—"

"Dammit to hell, girl. I wasn't' talking about apricots."

Her voice was soft, and her touch was gentle. She wrapped her arms around his waist, laid her cheek against his backbone, and hugged.

"Welcome home, Cole Brownfield. You were missed."

As he'd thought before, he wondered, *How the hell do you stay mad with someone who won't fight back?*

His hands caught her wrists, unlocked them, and turned himself in her arms. He pressed her face against his heartbeat, wrapped his hands in her hair, and inhaled. She smelled of soap and flowers...and those goddamned apricots. And he'd never been so glad to be home in his life.

"Is that so?" he asked. "Well, just for the record, I missed being here, too."

"Are you hungry?"

Hell, yes, I'm hungry. I'm starving for you, Deborah Randall.

"A little. I'm more tired than hungry."

She leaned back, using his arms for a brace, and took one long look at the shadows in his eyes. She swiped at the hopelessly straight hair brushing his forehead and gave his cheek a pat.

"Go shower...shave...change. I'll have something ready when you are."

It was the best deal he'd ever been offered. "I'll be right back."

He never made it. Debbie had seen the exhaustion. She suspected what might occur. She'd been right.

She stood outside his closed door, listening. She heard the first shoe hit the floor. Seconds later, after a soft grunt, the other. It was quiet. For long moments, she heard nothing. And then the soft, gentle sound of an exhausted snore.

She pushed open the door. He was flat on his back, one arm slung across his eyes, the other flung across his pillow. His legs dangling from the bed. She went to get Morgan.

"I need help," she said.

Morgan didn't ask. He followed. And when he saw his son and the state he was in, tears threatened.

"He works too damned hard," Morgan said as Debbie motioned for him to pull while she pushed.

Together they managed to get Cole all the way onto the bed.

"He'll sleep better if we could get his jeans off, but I'll settle for unbuttoning the top buttons instead."

Morgan nodded and complied as Debbie went to the linen closet and retrieved a lightweight blanket. It was hot outside, but inside, the air-conditioning kept everything at a comfortable seventy-two degrees. Asleep, that sometimes became too cool for comfort.

She pulled the soft blue blanket over Cole, resisted the urge to lie down beside him, and settled for a pat on his arm instead.

"Come on," she said. "He can always eat later. I don't think he's slept since he left."

The tears were thick in her voice and in her eyes, but Morgan wisely refrained from mentioning the fact. He had to. He was too full of emotion himself to bring it up.

Cole slept the clock around. When he awoke, he could smell coffee and the aroma of freshly baked oatmeal cookies, and he could smell himself. He groaned, rolled over and off his bed, stripping his jeans and shirt as he walked.

The shower came on just as his last item of clothing

came off. He walked beneath the jetting spray, reveling in the sting of water yet to warm.

The last thing he remembered was walking in on Debbie kissing his brother. And he vaguely remembered holding her and promising something about "being right back." He grimaced as he reached for the soap and shampoo. It was obvious that he'd never made it.

He stood beneath the shower until the water got hot and then until the water ran cold because he'd emptied the tank. He exited the stall, grabbed a bath towel, and wrapped it around him as he walked back into his room to get some clean underwear.

A steaming cup of hot coffee and a plate with three cookies, still warm from the oven, sat on his bedside table. Startled, he half expected to see Debbie's teasing face peeking out from around some door. But she was nowhere in sight. He sank down on the bed, unmindful of his still-wet body, and inhaled two cookies before he remembered to chew. The last, he savored with the coffee, thinking that a guy could get used to this kind of treatment.

He dried and dressed, gave his hair a half swipe with a comb, and gathered up his empty cup and plate.

"Got a refill?"

Debbie turned at the sink. She dropped the potato she was peeling back into the bowl and stuffed her hands into her apron pockets to keep from throwing them around his neck.

"You look better," she said softly.

"I hope to hell I do," he teased. "I saw myself just before I walked into the shower. It even scared me."

She grinned. Buddy walked into the kitchen.

"Debbie made cookies," he announced.

Cole nodded, holding up his empty plate.

"Chocolate chip is *my* favorite," Buddy said.

Cole privately thought that his brother was nuts. He knew good and well that he'd just eaten oatmeal and raisin. He should. They were his favorite.

"Debbie made oatmeal and raisin," Buddy continued.

Cole's eyebrows shot up toward his hairline. Suddenly, he, too, was beginning to understand Buddy's odd manner of conversation. Especially when he saw Debbie blush at Buddy's last remark. And he knew that Buddy was explaining, in the only way Buddy knew how, that the kiss Debbie had given him had been innocent.

"I know, Robert Allen," Cole said. "You can go to your room now."

Buddy grinned. "I'm going to my room now," he echoed.

They stared at each other and then burst out laughing. It was impossible not to. And for the first time since he and Debbie had parted company after their day at the beach, he felt happy inside himself.

"I'm starving," he said. "What have you got to eat...besides oatmeal-and-raisin cookies?"

"Sit," Debbie ordered. "It won't take a minute.

I've got anything you could possibly want." She began rummaging through the refrigerator.

He watched the seductive sway of her body as she moved around the kitchen. His insides twisted themselves into pretzels, but he ignored the twinges. "Yes, Little Red. You certainly have."

Cole and Debbie had come to an unspoken agreement. They'd agreed to disagree on certain issues yet to be resolved. Thankfully, it left the temperature in the Brownfield household somewhere back in the range of normalcy. No more frozen looks or cold shoulders between them, just lots of midnight dips in a chilly pool for Cole and sleepless nights for Debbie. Nothing serious and nothing that couldn't be remedied…when the time was right.

But it took a routine call on a routine day for Cole to realize that time was not always going to be on his side…or waiting. Time had a way of running out when you least expected it. And for Debbie, it almost ran out for good.

"Just drop me off at the mall," Debbie said. "You go on to your appointment, and I'll take a cab home when I'm through."

Morgan hesitated in the mall parking lot. It was broad daylight. Debbie was a grown woman, even if she was tiny. Women shopped alone all over the world…everywhere, every day. He knew he was just being overprotective. But he couldn't help it. This tiny female had come to mean a lot to all of them, especially his eldest son.

"Well…" he began.

"Come on, Morgan. If I go with you and sit and wait, then you're simply going to have to come back with me and sit and wait some more. None of that makes any sense, now does it?"

He sighed and grinned. "You've got me there." And then he pointed his finger in her face. "But when you're ready to come home, call a cab from inside the mall, and then wait at the door until you see it drive up. Don't stand outside. You'll simply be an easy target for some thug."

"Okay, okay," she agreed. "But don't worry. This is no different from any big mall anywhere. I've survived Quail Springs Mall in Oklahoma City. I've survived the Galleria in Dallas. Surely I can survive Laguna Beach's Village Fair."

He nodded. "Do you have enough money?" And then before she could refuse, he thrust several twenties in her hand. "Don't argue with me. It's either this, or you come with me."

She leaned over and kissed his cheek. "See you back at the house."

He waited until she was inside and then drove off, thankful that this little bit of nothing had come into their lives and thankful that he could now maneuver around more or less on his own.

Two hours and several shops later, Debbie looked at her watch in surprise. It was later than she thought.

She'd better hurry. If Morgan got home before she did, he'd send out the troops—or Buddy—to look for her. It would be hard to guess which would cause more commotion, an entire battalion or one absentminded computer genius.

She grinned as she hurried out of the store, her small sack of makeup clutched in her hand. She made a mad dash for the escalator. There was one more shop she wanted to visit. The morning paper had mentioned a sale.

Her foot caught the step as it unfolded and began its ascent toward the next level. She looked up, partly out of habit, partly to see where she was going, and then forgot to breathe.

On the next aisle, coming toward her, coming down, was a young man. His face was familiar…too familiar. And the last time she'd seen it…he'd been flipping off the world and stealing an old woman's purse.

Thomas Holliday was bored. It was why he'd come to the mall. He'd been here most of the day, filching what he could when he could and laughing to himself at not being caught. He was invincible. He was a stud. And tonight, after he picked up Nita Warren, he'd show her what being a stud meant.

And then he saw the woman. At first, he couldn't place her…and then his belly turned and sweat ran. He reacted before he thought.

The escalator was almost empty. Only one woman

with two small children behind her...no one behind him. He could tell she was nervous. That told him she'd recognized him, too. It made him feel strong.

Debbie looked up, and then she turned and looked behind her. If the woman and her children hadn't been there, she'd have backtracked. Now, it was impossible. There was only one thing left for her to do. She'd ride up and call Cole. And then everything went black.

Thomas's fist shot out. It connected with her chin as his hand yanked at the bag on her shoulder. But something went wrong. The purse wouldn't come loose. And then he noticed that she had it over her head and then across her shoulder. And he'd just knocked her out!

She went limp and loose as an uncoiled rope as the stairs carried her out of his reach. He cursed and ran down the stairs and out of the mall, with the woman and her children's shrieks ringing in his ears.

"Hey, partner," Rick yelled as Cole came out of the washroom at the service station. "We just got a call to go out to Village Fair Mall. Isn't that close to your house? The call said a lady requires your services." He smiled and leered, giving his best Groucho Marx imitation.

"Just shut up and drive," Cole grinned.

He slid into the passenger side of the unmarked unit. It had been a slow day. They'd simply been following up on some leads, eliminating the bad, taking note of the ones that might lead to something more.

They weren't far from their destination. It didn't take long to get there. It took less time to park. It was not in their nature to dawdle, even when something was not earmarked an emergency. But the emergency quickly presented itself as Cole and Rick walked into the small security office and Debbie stood up from the chair in which she'd been sitting.

"Cole."

The quiver in her voice was nearly his undoing. But his training stood him in good stead. He saw the new bruise on her face, and the color receding from her face. He caught her just before she fainted.

Chapter 5

"What the—?" Rick Garza took one look at his partner's face and the woman he caught in his arms. The fear in Cole's voice told him the rest.

"It's Debbie," Cole said.

Cole searched her body for further signs of injury beyond what he could already see. The obvious ones were enough to make him sick. He was desperately trying to maintain his rational thinking when all he wanted to do was vent the rage that was threatening to overwhelm him. Someone had hurt his lady.

"*Your* Debbie?" Rick was beginning to understand. Cole had talked of nothing else since her arrival. He was either constantly ticked off because of what she'd done or worried because of something she hadn't.

Cole nodded. *My Debbie!* He shuddered as he lowered her onto a sofa in the outer office of the security department. The mall manager hovered, concerned for the young woman's welfare, panicked that they might be sued.

"What happened?" Cole asked. He was all business. And it was then that he noticed the woman and two children sitting at a table in another room, obviously giving some sort of statement. He caught the look in Rick's eyes and nodded. As usual, they'd read each other's mind.

Rick touched Cole's arm. "I'll see what that's all about," he said, and hurried into the other room.

Cole knelt at Debbie's side. The manager quickly dumped everything he knew about the incident in the officer's lap.

"All we know is that she was riding up an escalator and someone coming down on the opposite side tried to rob her. The woman in the other room saw everything."

Cole's mouth thinned and his eyes narrowed as he carefully felt for Debbie's pulse. Everything about him seemed cool and methodical. He gave a good imitation of calm under fire. What he wanted to do was hit something…or someone.

"Have you called an ambulance? Did the woman say what Debbie was hit with?" His dark eyes raked the purpling bruise on her chin. "Was it some sort of a weapon or…?"

"Miss Randall wouldn't let us call an ambulance. She just wanted us to call you. She said she was fine.

Actually, she seemed to be until you walked in." The manager shrugged, as if to say it was out of his hands. "As for the witness, she said the boy just doubled up his fist and swung. Couldn't believe what she was seeing. Then he tried to get her purse but was unsuccessful."

"Hell!" Cole's single expletive said it all.

"I've got a copy of her statement," Rick said as he came back into the room. "She thinks she can identify the man. She's volunteered to go down and look at some mug shots." He looked down at the tiny woman lying so pale and still. "Come on, buddy. Let's get her to a hospital. We'll beat an ambulance if I drive."

Cole looked up, read the concern on his partner's face, and nodded. Debbie was starting to come around.

"Debbie?" Cole's voice was soft and low as he brushed her hair away from her forehead and tried not to look at the bruise on her face and the cut on her lip. "Honey....can you hear me?"

She moaned. Her eyelids fluttered, and her fingers began to twitch as she tightened her grip onto the only anchor she could find...Cole.

"It was him." Her speech was slurred, her eyesight blurry as her makeshift bed tried to go into orbit inside the tiny office.

"Him? Who, honey?" Cole asked.

Her heart thumped as she saw Cole and struggled to sit. *He's here! Thank God!*

"The man from the beach...the one who stole Flor-

ence Goldblum's purse…remember?'' Her fingers dug
into his wrist.

Cole's expression froze. *My God!* ''You
mean…that day…you saw his face?''

''Yes. I thought you knew,'' she whispered.
''Didn't you?''

''Not really. I was already running, remember?''

Debbie closed her eyes and swallowed. The words
came out in a rush. ''At the beach…when it happened…he saw me watching him. Today…when we
met on the escalator…I don't know who was more
surprised, me or him.''

''You mean he knows who you are?'' The growl
was deep, and threatening. Debbie had to look up just
to assure herself that Cole's anger wasn't directed at
her.

''I guess. At least, he knows my face.'' And then
she moaned as the sofa took another turn around the
room.

Cole took a deep breath. He nodded to Rick, again
the need for conversation unnecessary. The man had
to be found. After what he'd done today, it was obvious that he didn't like witnesses.

''Be still, honey,'' he cautioned. ''We're going to
take you to the hospital. I'm going to carry you. I don't
want you to move unnecessarily. Just let me do all the
work, okay?''

She started to nod and then grabbed her head and
moaned. Rick had seen that look before. He reached

for the nearest trash can and shoved it beneath her chin just as the nausea caught her unawares.

"Possible concussion," Cole muttered. "Maybe we'd better call an ambulance."

"You get her. I'll get another can. It won't be the first time someone threw up in the car. Remember that time I got a bad burger? I was sick for a week."

Cole tried to smile. But he was too worried to manage more than a grimace. "I owe you."

"I won't let you forget."

"I talked to your dad," Rick said as he walked back into the emergency room.

Cole nodded. He hadn't taken his eyes off Debbie's whereabouts since their arrival. "Thanks," he muttered.

The doctor had assured him, after a quick but thorough examination, that she was suffering only a mild concussion, some contusions, and a few scratches. Cole had watched the white knit shirt come over her head, winced at the evidence of more bruising on her shoulder that had probably been a result of her fall, and tried not to curse.

The doctor had then insisted on privacy, at which Cole promptly balked. But the doctor had been firm. And Cole now sat outside the curtained-off area, listening to Debbie's shaky voice explaining the circumstances of her injuries.

"She's going to be just fine," Rick encouraged him.

"Well, I'm not," Cole said harshly. "I just realized

that I'm capable of murder. Being an officer sworn to uphold the law, it's not a thing of which I'm pleased to learn about myself. It's just a goddamned fact.''

Rick's hand gripped his shoulder in a gesture of understanding. He knew exactly what Cole was feeling. If it had been his Tina, he'd have felt the same.

''I'm going to head on back to the P.D.—let them know what we've been up to today and make your apologies, so to speak. You've got time off coming. Why don't you take a few days?''

''Past getting her home and into bed, I don't know what the hell I'm going to do, but I doubt that I'll sit on my thumbs. I want to make sure the son of a bitch who did this gets caught. Have you heard anything more about the witness?''

Rick shook his head. ''But I'll find out and give you a call later this evening. How's that?''

''I'd appreciate it,'' Cole said. ''Did Dad say he'd be here soon?''

''From the sound of his voice when I called, if he could have flown, he'd already be here. Sounded really worried.''

''He likes her a lot.'' Cole looked toward the curtain. ''So does Buddy.''

''And so do you, my man. If you can't admit it to me, at least admit it to yourself.''

Cole wouldn't look up, but the words came out. ''What if she can't handle my job, Rick? I won't give it up. And I've seen too many marriages go to hell because of the crazy work schedules and the constant danger. I wouldn't be able to face losing her."

"If you don't give yourselves a chance, you've already lost her, buddy. Ever think about that?"

Cole buried his face in his hands. Rick slapped him on the back and made a quick exit. He waved at Cole's father as he came hobbling into the hallway and directed him to where Cole was sitting.

"I knew I shouldn't have left her alone," Morgan said as he sank down onto the chair beside his son. "If I hadn't, none of this would have happened. It's all my fault."

Cole frowned. "That's not exactly what you've spent the last thirty-odd years trying to teach me, mister. I thought you always said that whatever was going to happen, would happen, no matter how much hindsight was applied."

Morgan shrugged and then smiled. "You pick the oddest times to remember my sermons." He heard Debbie's voice. "Is she going to be all right?" The worry was back in his voice.

Cole looked at the man who was so like himself, and smiled. "Yeah, Dad. She's going to be just fine. Got a bump on her head and a bruise on her chin, but she's already worrying about who's going to cook dinner tonight. I just heard the doctor tell her to order out. What do you bet we eat Chinese again? All those cute little boxes…remember?"

"My God," Morgan sighed. "The resilience of youth."

* * *

"We'll take turns looking in on her," Buddy offered. It was a major concession for him that he would even consider leaving his computer components for a human being.

"I don't usually go to sleep until after the Carson— I mean, the Leno show. I could do it," Morgan offered.

"Thanks. But I'll tend to her," Cole said. "It only makes sense. She's right across the hall. I used to look in on Lily when she was sick, remember?"

Morgan remembered. He also remembered the look he'd seen on Cole's face when he'd first walked into the emergency room. It had been somewhere between desperate and devastated. He was just thankful that Debbie was not seriously hurt. Cole could not have handled anything worse.

"Whatever you think, son," he said. "But if you do need help, you know where we are."

Cole nodded. "The doctor said just to keep an eye on her, make sure she doesn't sleep too soundly or do too much right at first, and—" he shrugged and frowned "—wait for the bruises to fade."

"Where is she now?" Buddy asked. "I could see if she wants something to eat. Maybe some yogurt or—"

"That's great, Buddy," Cole smiled. "She's in her room. Why don't you knock on her door and then ask? I don't think she's doing anything but lying down right now."

Buddy grinned, happy that he'd thought of something useful, and made a dash for the hallway.

"Did you ever think you'd see the day when a woman would get Buddy out of his precious room?" Morgan was grinning.

"No. And it's a good thing that he doesn't see her as a woman. He sees her more as an extension of Lily. I'd hate to have to fight my own brother for her."

Morgan's mouth dropped. He turned and stared, but Cole disappeared into the kitchen, ignoring the bombshell he'd handed his father.

She was sleeping peacefully on her side, rolled up in a tiny ball with the sheets wrapped around and under her like a swaddled baby.

Cole couldn't decide whether to curse or cry. He did neither. Instead, he simply walked over to the side of her bed, lightly felt across her forehead for signs of fever, and sighed with relief as his palm slid over cool, smooth skin.

The urge to unwrap and straighten her covers was strong, but he knew it would be futile. Two hours ago he'd tried and was now staring at the results. If she'd been bagged and labeled by experts, she wouldn't have been packaged any better. He turned and walked away.

Debbie felt his touch, the sigh on her cheek as he leaned over and brushed her forehead with his lips, and then heard his footsteps as he left her alone... again.

She didn't move or indicate by any means that she'd been aware of his presence. Not now, or the other times he'd come into her room when he should have been getting his own rest.

She blinked back tears. When he thought she wasn't looking, he was so damned gentle it made her heart hurt. Why couldn't he admit that what was between them was more than just casual caring? Why wouldn't he face the fact that they were in love?

The first time she'd seen him standing beneath a shade tree at the Longren Ranch, a plate full of barbecue in one hand and a beer in the other, laughing at something someone had said, she'd been lost.

He was so different from the men with whom she'd grown up. Besides his being from California—and where she came from, that counted as another planet—besides his being a cop, which took her exactly five minutes to discover, besides his being Lily's oldest and best-loved brother—besides all that, he had secrets.

She'd recognized them instantly. They hung just behind the darkest pair of eyes she'd ever seen. And she could tell that the secrets weren't all good. There was a world of sadness behind his laugh. It reeked of too many lonely hours and too many ugly sights. Yes, in the space of five minutes, Deborah Jean Randall had seen all that and fallen in love.

Now here she was, half a country away, after being whomped by a creep who made a habit of preying on helpless women and nearly being eaten alive by a moving, metal staircase, she was next door to the man of her dreams, and he wouldn't let her sleep.

Debbie rolled over, winced as she mashed a sore spot, and stretched, trying to find a comfortable place to settle. Soon, she'd drifted back to sleep to the tune of the floorboard creaking in the room across the hall.

It was halfway to morning. Midnight had come and gone like a bandit, stealing away whatever rest Cole had been trying to find. He cursed the moonlight shining through his window. Cursed fate for what had happened to Debbie. Cursed the creep who was still out there unapprehended. Cursed everything and everyone except what mattered.

He was not where he belonged. His heart had been telling him that for hours. Finally, in sleepless desperation, he rolled off his bed. Moonbeams danced across his bare body, shadowing the hard curves and flat planes of his well-toned torso. He pulled on a pair of red jogging shorts and started across the hall. Just for one more look. Just to make sure she was still alive…and breathing.

Debbie heard the floorboard creak. She groaned as it woke her and tried to burrow back down into the covers. He was up again. If she could just locate that comfortable spot…but it was gone. And Cole was here.

He leaned over, peering through the shadows, trying to see her face—listening to her breathing—just to assure himself that it was gentle and regular.

"For the love of God, Cole Brownfield," Debbie muttered. "You won't let either of us rest. If you can't calm down and let me sleep and trust the fact that my next breath won't be my last, then you have my permission to crawl in beside me and listen to me breathe."

She'd startled him. And then he smiled to himself. He should have known it would take more than this to get her down. He looked at the shadowy contours of her sleepy face, saw the invitation, and knew that it hadn't been far from his thoughts since he'd brought her home.

"Do you pull covers?" he asked as he began to unwrap her.

"You'll soon see," she muttered, and allowed him to straighten the bed.

It took every ounce of willpower he owned, but he crawled in and settled down. For one long moment, neither spoke.

Debbie had issued the invitation out of frustration. He had accepted it out of need. But when his long arm gently snaked beneath her head and pulled her toward him, she sighed. There! She'd found that comfortable spot again, after all. She should have known where it was. It was next to his heart.

Cole gently wrapped her, covers and all, and held her. Long after he'd felt her relax, long after he heard her breathing slow and soften, he watched and he listened. And he fell in love.

* * *

"Good morning, honey."

Debbie opened her eyes, stared up into the faces of two extra Brownfields who were grinning down at her, and stretched and smiled. Her arm hit the other pillow and she jerked, suddenly remembering her bed partner. She breathed a quiet sigh of relief. He was gone. It would have been awkward explaining his presence.

"Cole made us get up," Buddy said.

Morgan grinned. "He got an early call. He said to bring your food to you. I'll just set it on the bed here beside you. After you've washed up, you can dig in."

He watched her wince as she tried to smile around the bruise on her chin. A dark anger, similar to the one his son was wearing, began to simmer. He'd give a lot for an hour alone with the man who'd done this. "Can you manage on your own? Maybe you need some help getting out of bed? Are you sore?"

"Yes. No. Yes."

Morgan grinned again. Their old Debbie was back. "I get the picture. Come on, Buddy. We're in the way."

"When it's time, I'll fix lunch," Buddy announced.

Morgan rolled his eyes as they made an exit. "No one wants a diet of pure sugar but you son. I think we'd better just wait and see if anyone even wants to eat. What do you say?"

He hated to discourage the first normal thing his son had offered to do in nearly five years, but he didn't think any of them was ready for ice cream decorated with dollops of peanut butter and sprinkled with Fruit Loops.

Debbie wanted to laugh. But she wasn't sure her mouth would take the punishment so she settled for a small smile instead. With a little effort and a lot of moaning, she made it into the bathroom and into a pair of shorts and a huge oversized T-shirt that had belonged to her brother, Douglas. The less that touched her body, the better she felt.

She crawled back into bed, dug into the lukewarm toast, the still-hot coffee, and saved the strawberry jelly for Buddy. Bland food was all her stomach could tolerate.

"Yes, darling, I love you, too." Debbie smiled carefully, tucked a stray curl behind her ear, and pivoted on bare feet as she heard someone walk into the kitchen behind her. Her eyebrows raised at the expression on Cole's face, but she continued her conversation, knowing that he'd probably misinterpret it and figuring that it would be good for his blood pressure when he did.

Cole wanted to rip that phone out of her hand, demand to know who the hell she was calling "darling," and then tell them to get one of their own. This one was his.

He caught himself short. *What the hell is wrong with me? I've given her nothing but walls. What makes me think she wants to climb over?*

His eyes narrowed as he watched her body dancing

beneath that oversized shirt. He knew she was wearing next to nothing and the thought made him hot...and hard.

"Yes, I promise," she said. "And I'm really having a good time. No. I won't forget. I'm proud of you, and thanks for calling. Yes, I'll look forward to it."

She hung up with a secretive smile and turned. The wall was behind her. She decided to use it for a prop and waited for Cole to ask. He didn't disappoint her.

"Who was that?" His question wasn't friendly.

"Douglas."

He waited. Nothing more was forthcoming. And it was not enough.

"So...you're going to make me ask, aren't you, Little Red?"

She shrugged. "I don't know what you mean." And then her conscience tugged. Last night, after he'd finally let her sleep, had been the best night of her life. She wanted more like it...and often. "Douglas is my brother. He got my number from Lily. He got a promotion and his company is moving him to L.A. Small world, huh?"

"He doesn't know you were hurt, does he?"

Debbie ducked her head and shrugged, then winced at the movement. "No need. I survived."

I don't know if I will. The bruise on her chin made him want to cry. Cole walked over, slipped her oversized T-shirt down, letting the neckline slide off her shoulder. Another bruise was revealed. He'd seen it in the E.R. It wasn't any less faint. Neither was the one on her chin. They were very vivid, very dark swatches of purple and green. The thought of that man—of anyone—hitting her with such savagery…

She looked up. The fury in his eyes made her shake. And she knew it was not directed at her. She pushed herself from the wall, wrapped her arms around his waist, and hugged him.

"I'm okay," she whispered.

"Well, I'm not," he muttered. He didn't know what hurt more: his feelings, for not somehow being able to prevent this when he was supposed to be a cop who took care of people, or his unrelieved libido, for the night he'd spent holding her in his arms.

She loved holding him. Even if it made him nervous. Even if he hadn't instigated the action. His blue jeans were rough against her bare legs, his striped shirt soft against her cheek. He smelled good. All lemony and woodsy. And he felt even better. He was so big and so hard in so many interesting places and— Her hands ceased their movement beneath his jacket. She looked up and forgot what she'd been about to say.

"It's my gun."

She yanked her hands back from around him as if she'd just put them on a snake. It was the leather shoulder holster that she'd felt. And the look on his face told her that she'd done the wrong thing by being shocked.

Cole saw it. He'd been waiting for something like this for weeks. Ever since her arrival, he'd known that someday something was bound to happen that would prove to him that a relationship between them wouldn't work. He'd been certain that his occupation would be abhorred, that his daily lifestyle would be a problem. He'd been waiting…and he was sick to his stomach that he'd been right.

"Well, I know that," Debbie finally said. "I just wasn't expecting it. After all, it's not like I've ever seen you completely dressed that many times anyway."

Her statement hadn't been what he'd expected. As usual, she'd caught him off guard. And her reminder that last night he'd had little to nothing on as they slept the rest of the night away took him aback.

He still wasn't certain that she was revealing her true feelings. There were women he'd known who'd been appalled that he carried a gun. There had been others who'd been turned on by the fact. He wanted someone in between. He'd never found her. He didn't think she existed. At least, he'd believed that wholeheartedly until that damned cabby had dumped a lost tornado from Oklahoma on his doorstep. Now he wasn't so sure. In fact, he hadn't been sure about a thing since.

"I just stopped by to see how you're doing and to tell you that the witness at the mall identified the guy. At least, it's a tentative I.D. I wondered if you'd mind looking at a few pictures…?"

"Are you working on this case?" Debbie was surprised. "I thought you only worked on stuff involving narcotics."

"Not officially."

The tone and intensity of his voice told her more than his terse answer.

"Let's just say I have a…vested interest…in seeing that nothing else happens to you, lady."

Debbie nodded. "Then spread 'em," she mocked.

The look on his face was worth the pain she felt as she laughed. "I mean the pictures, you dork. What did you think, that I was going to frisk you?" She ran her finger down the buttons of his shirt and, when she got to his belt buckle, tapped it sharply with her nail. "That's your job, remember?"

"Hell's fire!"

She cocked her eyebrow, tried not to smile again, and waited for him to show her the pictures. He finally came to his senses, yanked an envelope out of his jacket pocket, and strung several photos on the kitchen table.

"This one," Debbie said quickly. It hadn't taken long to pick out that belligerent face beneath long blond hair.

"Sure?"

"Very. And I can't believe I didn't think to tell you I'd seen him. I guess I just assumed that, because I had, you did, too. If I'd had my wits about me, maybe none of this would've happened."

Cole slid the pictures back in the envelope and headed for the phone. When someone answered, his comment was short and sweet. "It's him. She made a positive I.D." He nodded as he listened, and then quickly disconnected. "They're putting out an APB. Maybe if we catch him, we'll get the rest of that snatch-and-grab gang operating at the beach."

"Good. I'd hate to think about any more nice people like Florence Goldblum getting hurt. The next one might not be as lucky as Florence."

"Lucky?"

Debbie smiled. "Yes, lucky. If you hadn't been there, no one would have retrieved her bag in time to get her medicine." She punched him lightly in the stomach. "And you know it, tough guy."

"Oh, there'll always be a next time. The world's full of creeps like that."

Debbie hugged him, purposely resting her cheek on the bulge of his holster just to prove that it didn't shock her by its presence. "And the world's just as full of nice guys...like you."

His arms tightened, and then he quickly released them, remembering her injuries.

"I've got to get back. I just wanted to make sure—"

"I'm fine. However, I can't promise what condition I'll be in by bedtime."

He frowned. "Why?"

"Buddy wants to cook dinner."

Cole leaned his head back and laughed. He looked down at her face, saw the barely concealed distress, and laughed again.

"I'll try not to be late," he chuckled. "However, if

I am, don't feel obligated to hold dinner for me. I'll just grab a bite somewhere else.''

"You're lying and you know it." She sighed. "For two cents, I'd go with you. I don't know if my stomach can stand four courses of sweets."

Cole's voice was gentle as he leaned down and swept a quick kiss across her forehead.

"For less than that, I'd take you with me." His dark eyes raked the slender curves beneath her floppy shirt. And then he shrugged. "But duty calls, at least it will, if I don't get myself back in gear. Take care, girl."

Debbie's tone was light, but the shadows in her eyes told him that she dreaded to see him go. "You, too," she said, and absently patted the holster beneath his jacket.

He grabbed her hand, holding it gently but firmly as he made her look at him. He needed to see that the fear wasn't there. He had to assure himself that she wasn't about to fly to pieces over where he was going.

She pulled her hand away and gave the jacket one more pat.

"Just checking," she said. "Wouldn't want you to leave without all your…bulges in place." She made a theatrical leer at the one behind his zipper and then grinned as he blushed.

"I'm already gone," Cole muttered. "Hell, it's safer out on the streets than it is here with you."

"Maybe," Debbie said. "But here, you wouldn't need a gun. I'd go easy."

God almighty! Cole made a beeline for the door. He

didn't have time to pursue this interesting line of questioning. And, he had no desire to return to work in any kind of shape that would require explanations. He ignored the ache behind his zipper and focused on the one in his heart. When he got back, Deborah Jean Randall owed him more than answers. He'd been teased and tortured past his limit.

Chapter 6

That laugh! Cole pivoted, nearly dropping his hot dog and cola as he stared at the woman across the street.

It was Debbie!

Pleasure surfaced at the unexpected sighting. He started to yell a hello when a man came out of the men's clothing store behind her and gave her a kiss.

His hands knotted. Lunch was instantly forgotten and so was the fact that he was still holding it. His fingers squeezed into fists and into his meal. His wiener went one direction, his bun the other. He was left holding the chili...and the bag.

What in hell? He'd never seen that man before, and he'd have sworn that Debbie didn't know anyone in Laguna Beach besides his family. If she did, she certainly hadn't mentioned it.

He looked down at the mess in his hands and cursed softly.

"Here, buddy," the vendor said, handing him a handful of napkins. "Looks like you might be needing these."

Cole took them, nodded his thanks, and stared at the back end of that disappearing taxi.

"Want another?" the vendor asked, hoping to make another sale. Cole made a dash for his car. The vendor shrugged.

Cole spun out into traffic and began following the taxi's retreat. Several minutes elapsed before the taxi finally came to another stop.

He frowned. A clothing store? Again? Surely Debbie hasn't been suckered into buying clothes for some gigolo? He couldn't imagine her being suckered into anything. But she was a stranger here, and in Cole's line of work, odder things had happened.

They exited the cab. Cole watched the taxi drive away. Obviously they intended to spend some time inside. He frowned again and tightened his grip on the steering wheel as the broad-shouldered young man wrapped his arm solicitously around Debbie's shoulder and escorted her inside.

He was nearly six feet tall and stocky. Cole took careful note of the fact that he couldn't possibly be older than his early twenties. Dark brown hair. And no tan! He wasn't local. That much was obvious. Someone with that many muscles would also have sported a tan. The two were synonymous in California, especially with body builders.

Cole thought about just getting out of his car, going across the street, and introducing himself. Then he thought again. How would he explain that he'd known where she was? He didn't want to admit to her—or anyone else—that he'd been following her. It smacked of insecurity. *I'm damn sure not insecure...I don't think.*

He frowned, settled himself into a more comfortable position, and fixed his sight on the front door. Sooner or later, they'd have to come out. When they did, he'd decide what to do next.

Doug Randall kept one eye on his sister and the other on the sales clerk. If that prissy guy brought out any more coordinating pinks and greens, he was leaving. He'd wear white shirts to work every day before he'd button on something sissy.

When Doug wasn't looking, Debbie grinned. It was something to see him well groomed and successful. She'd spent too many years worrying if he'd ever amount to anything other than a sometime mechanic and a full-time biker. He'd been Clinton, Oklahoma's, most avid proponent of black leather and Harleys. It had nearly been her undoing.

Somewhere between the age of seventeen and now, Doug had grown up and out of that phase. She'd been constantly thankful ever since.

"You think you're going to like your new job?"

Debbie watched her brother's glare send the salesman scurrying back to the racks for another color of shirt.

"The job's not new, Deb. Just the location."

Douglas frowned. She was so pale. And when he'd first seen the bruises on her face, he'd been livid. He'd been all ready to go out and search the streets of Laguna Beach for the creep until she'd calmly informed him that there was already an entire police force on her side. She'd claimed they didn't need his help. It hadn't made him feel much better.

"You could come with me," he persisted. It had been the subject of most of their conversation the entire afternoon. "I've already got a two-bedroom apartment in what I'm told is the 'better' part of L.A." He grinned wryly. "If L.A. has a better part, I've yet to see it."

"You're too country, Douglas. There's much to be said for city living." She ignored his frown. "And for the last time, I'm not moving in with my little brother—" she raised her eyebrows as he flexed his arms in a none-too-subtle reminder of who was really the smaller "—no matter what he says. Besides, think of your love life."

He flushed and grinned. "I don't have one…yet."

"Exactly," she said. "And I'd like to see how fast it progressed with your sister in the next room."

"Still—" he persisted.

"Still nothing," she argued. "Now hush. The clerk's coming back. Oooh, Douglas, I think I like that one." She pointed to the shirt the sales clerk was carrying.

"It still looks sorta pink to me," Douglas frowned.

"Oh no," the clerk said, "this is just a shade darker than mauve and two shades lighter than raspberry. It's in vogue. Trust me."

"Sounds like I should eat it, not wear it," Douglas growled. And then they both laughed at the look on the clerk's face.

"We'll take it," Debbie said.

Cole was furious. After the clothing stores, they'd gone into a shoe store and then a specialty shop that carried elegant men's accessories. He'd parked close enough to watch them take several expensive ties to the register and then watched as Debbie tried to pay for them.

What was the matter with her? When they came out of this store, he was making his move. He couldn't wait to see the look on her face when he walked up!

"Hey, Sis," Douglas Randall muttered. "I've just noticed that same damned car again. The last three places we've stopped, it's been outside. Once down the street, the last time across the street, and now there it's sitting right outside in plain sight."

"I know," she said, calmly matching ties to the shirts inside the sacks he was carrying.

"It might be that nut who hurt you. I've half a mind to—"

"It's Cole."

"It's who?" Then understanding dawned. "You mean that's the guy who—?"

"That's the one."

"What the hell you suppose he's doing?"

"Following me." She held up a tie. "What do you think? This print's not too fussy and it picks up the mauve pinstripe rather nicely, don't you agree?"

"Whatever." Doug shrugged. "I don't know ties from shoelaces, and you know it. Why do you think I came so far out of my way to get your advice?"

"To check up on me, just like that man out there. You're both just alike."

Her calm, matter-of-fact manner was impossible to argue with. Truth was the truth, no matter where you found it.

"Don't stare," Debbie cautioned. "We don't want to ruin his day by letting him find out he's been— what's the word?—'made.'"

Douglas looked down at his older sister with undisguised admiration. "You're something, Deb. I'm sure going to miss you."

"I love you, too," she said, and gave herself up to his hug. "Easy," she cautioned. "I'm still breakable." And then she sighed at the frown that appeared on her brother's face. She didn't want to get him started again. "Come on. This is enough. Besides, you'll miss your plane if you don't head to the airport soon."

"I've still got time," he argued. "I'll drop you off

at the Brownfields' and then head for the airport from there.''

"No way," she argued. "You won't have time. Trust me. We'll split up here. I'll take my own cab home. And that's final.''

"Well, I'm paying. And that's final.''

She grinned. "You sure grew up mean.''

"Just be glad I grew up," he said.

"Amen!" Debbie echoed. And they both laughed.

Cole was sick. She'd hugged him! *What did she do that for?* That did it. He wasn't waiting for them to come out. He was going in. *Hell's fire! The guy just handed her a wad of money!* He frowned as his belly turned another flop.

His hand was on the door when the call came in. There was a robbery going down. A silent alarm had just gone off in a jewelry store. Cole listened intently. That address was only a few blocks over. This confrontation with Debbie would have to wait.

He grabbed the mike, gave his location, and slapped his light on the dash. The red light began to revolve as he quickly pulled out into traffic. The run would be silent. No use warning the thief that he was on the way.

Debbie looked up just in time to see Cole leaving. She saw the red light, knew that duty had pulled him away from curiosity, and said a little prayer for his safety.

"Your cab's here," Douglas said. "Take care of yourself, honey. And I'll call you as soon as I get settled. Maybe you could come out for a visit real soon."

"Maybe," she said, but she wasn't committing herself to anything...except possibly Cole.

"I liked your brother," Morgan said, as they sat down to the supper table.

Debbie grinned. "Thanks, I do, too."

"He didn't like me," Buddy said.

She was shocked. "What makes you think that, Buddy?"

"I asked him if he wanted to see my new mouse, and he just stared at me and walked away."

Debbie tried not to laugh, but it was no use. "Oh Buddy, you're priceless," she chuckled. "The only mouse Douglas knows about has beady eyes, two little ears, and whiskers. Computers and their attachments are fairly new to him. I'm sure he didn't make the connection. If you'd only clarified yourself..."

Buddy's eyebrows notched perceptibly. "I always clarify myself—" he ducked his head and started in on his food, anxious to get past what he *had* to eat so he could get to what he *wanted* to eat, namely dessert "—given time."

"There's not enough time in my life to understand you, my son," Morgan teased. "Good thing I don't have to understand you to love you."

Buddy grinned and licked his spoon.

* * *

Cole turned into the driveway, stared for long, silent moments at the low-slung, ranch-style house and wished he was a thousand miles away. The last thing he wanted to do was go inside and listen to Debbie lie about where she'd been. He slammed the car door and had begun stomping toward the house when a thought struck him. *What if she doesn't even bother to lie? What if he's someone who really matters to her?*

Cole didn't like that thought at all.

He slammed the front door behind him.

"We're in here," Morgan called. "You're just in time for supper."

"Be there in a minute," he yelled, and made a quick run to his room to put up his gun and wash. He looked down at his clothes and decided he'd change while he was at it. There was chili all over his pant leg. Damn stuff would probably never come out.

Cole came into the kitchen, carrying an armload of clothes.

Debbie looked up. "Put those on the washer," she said. "I'll get to them after we eat."

"Don't bother," he said shortly. "I'll do them myself."

Morgan's eyebrows rose, but he wisely refrained from speaking.

Debbie smiled sweetly. "Whatever you say."

Cole dropped the laundry inside the laundry room

and then made a beeline for the table. Regardless of how angry he was, he was also hungry.

"I'm starving," he said. "Something smells good."

"Thank you," Debbie said. "It's Hungarian goulash."

"She made lemon pie."

"Thank you, Buddy. I'll save room." Cole managed to smile at his brother and gave his father the same weak excuse for a greeting. No use including them in his anger. It wasn't their fault the woman at the table was a hussy.

Cole scooped a double serving onto his plate, poured salad dressing onto his salad, and took the first bite. The aroma was good, but the flavor was better. *So the hussy can cook.*

"You really are hungry, aren't you?" Debbie's question was hooked, but Cole never even saw the barb coming until it was too late.

He nodded in agreement and continued to chew, savoring the meal along with intermittent gulps of cold, sweet tea made in honor of Buddy's palate.

"I don't suppose you ever did get a chance to eat."

He looked up and wondered where that remark came from. How would she know anything about his day? And then suspicion began to grow.

"Well, I did start to eat a—"

"Yes," Debbie said conversationally. "I watched your hot dog committing suicide, although we left before I noticed if you purchased another. However, I

don't see as how you had time because you came
along so quickly. Did you?''

Cole forgot to chew. "Did I what?"

"Did you buy another?"

He glared.

"Obviously not." Debbie smiled. "Here, honey,
have some more."

"I'm not your honey," he snarled. "You save that
for the hulk that kept mauling you all afternoon."

"Maul? Me? I think you misread the situation."
She lowered her voice to the sexiest possible tone and
let her eyelids flutter for effect. "I called that loving.
He's real good at it, too."

Cole slammed his fork down and had started to bolt
when Debbie stayed him with a motion of her hand.

"Please, don't leave on my account. I'm already
through. I think I'll go put your pants to soak."

Cole glared and tried not to blush. It was maddening
that his whole afternoon of sleuthing had been discov-
ered and that she'd stood by and let him make a fool
of himself.

"Why do you need to soak his pants?" Morgan
couldn't resist the question. He'd tried very hard to
stay out of the argument, but that statement had been
too loaded to miss.

"Chili's very hard to wash out," Debbie said. "I
think it's all that grease."

"Sugar washes out much better," Buddy offered.
"And it rarely stains."

"Shut up, Robert Allen."

Cole's glare did nothing to deter Buddy. When he was on a roll, he couldn't be stopped. "Douglas ate some of my pudding earlier, and it washed right off his shirt. Remember, Debbie?"

"I remember," she said, and headed for the washer.

"Who the hell is Douglas?" Cole asked, and then answered his own question as he remembered overhearing one of Debbie's phone calls. *Her brother! Oh hell! That was her brother!*

"Douglas is her—"

"Shut up," Cole snapped. And then he relented at the look of surprise on his brother's face. "Shut up, please," he said softly.

"Okay," Buddy said. "And Cole…"

"What?" he muttered, staring down at his half-finished meal.

"You need to get some extra rest tonight. I think you're about to suffer from burnout. I read somewhere that policemen suffer burnout twice as fast as—"

"Thank you, Buddy. I'll do that," Cole said.

Buddy nodded and made his escape, but not before serving himself with a double helping of lemon pie.

Debbie walked back into the kitchen. "They're soaking, but I'm not going to guarantee anything."

"I will," Cole said quietly.

Debbie turned.

"I guarantee that I will not jump to any more conclusions where you're concerned." His voice was low and defeated.

Morgan grinned and made his getaway.

Debbie walked over to the table and patted Cole's shoulder. She smiled when he leaned his head against her breasts and sighed with regret.

"Yes, you will, Cole. You can't help yourself. It's just a man thing. Now eat your food before it gets cold."

"Yes, ma'am," he said, and picked up his fork.

"Where are you going?" Cole asked. He aimed the television remote and hit the mute button. He took another look at Debbie's attire and turned the TV off completely. She was wearing her swimsuit beneath that oversized T-shirt.

"To swim. The sun's gone down and no one can see me."

"I don't get it. Why would you care if—" He remembered the bruises. "It doesn't matter, honey," he said softly. "They're only bruises, and they'll fade. Want me to come with you?"

She shrugged. "So, you've decided to speak to me?"

Cole flushed. "I never said I wouldn't," he argued. "It should be the other way around. I wouldn't blame you if you never spoke to me again. I don't know what I was thinking. I should have known better."

"Just what *did* you think, anyway?" Debbie asked.

Cole shrugged. "Nothing much, and it doesn't matter now." He waited for her reaction. When there was nothing but a look he didn't want to interpret, he asked, "So, do you want company or not?"

"If it's you, I always want company," she replied softly.

"I'll get my suit."

"Don't on my account," she said, and laughed as his face flushed two shades or red.

"If I had any sense, I'd go to bed," he muttered.

"You're the boss," Debbie teased. "If you don't swim, then bed it is. In fact, that sounds much more interesting than—"

"Get in the damn water, woman," he warned. "Get in and get wet before I change my mind...and yours."

This time, it was Debbie who blushed. She headed for the door.

"Ooh," Debbie sighed. "Now I know how Morgan feels when he does his water therapy. It hurts so good."

Cole's eyes darkened. He'd just put an entirely different connotation on what it took to hurt good. And it had nothing to do with swimming. He stood at the side of the pool and watched the measured control of her movements.

"Are you very stiff?" His question was gruff, but Debbie heard the concern.

"It's not so bad now. The bruises are fading pretty fast."

"Take off the shirt," Cole said.

"But I look so...spotty," she objected, trying to laugh away her embarrassment.

"Spotty is my favorite color," Cole said. "There's

no one else around. Be comfortable. You can't enjoy your swim with that long, wet shirt wrapped around your legs."

It didn't take any more urging. Debbie paddled across the pool until she could touch bottom. Then she began fighting the water's pull against the wet, clingy jersey knit. She was fighting a losing battle.

"I need help."

Cole kicked off his deck shoes and slipped into the pool. His long, lithe body cut a silent wake through the clear blue water. Debbie watched, fascinated.

"Don't fight it," Cole said as he reached beneath the surface and grasped the hem of the shirt. "Let me do all the work."

Debbie nodded and tried not to wince as he maneuvered her arm out of the clinging sleeve.

"Sorry, Little Red," Cole whispered. "One more sleeve does it." He pulled at the fabric, stretching it as much as possible before pulling it over her head. "There," he said. "Now you're free."

She wanted to laugh, but tears were too close to the surface. *Free? I'll never be free again as long as I live, Cole.* "Thanks," she managed to say. "That feels much better."

It doesn't look better, Cole thought. The bruises were dark-purple and green swatches on the fragile satin surface of her skin. In spite of his intentions to remain neutral during this swim, he couldn't resist a touch.

His fingertips feathered the darkest spot on her

shoulder and then traced a path through the droplets of water clinging to her skin.

Debbie shivered. Cole jerked his hand back.

"Cold?" He had a remedy for that, but he didn't think she was up to it.

"Not really," she said. "Just…oh, I don't know…I guess I've got the willies."

He laughed unexpectedly, lustily. "You have the most unique repertoire of euphemisms I've ever heard."

Debbie grinned. "Have I just been made fun of? Surely you jest. I can't believe that you've never heard of the willies."

Cole splashed her lightly, playfully responding to her attack on his command of the English language.

"You show me the definition in Webster's dictionary, and I'll…I'll cook dinner tomorrow. What exactly are…*willies?*"

Debbie cupped her hands, scooped up a handful of water, and let it trickle sensuously through her fingers onto his broad chest. When it had run its course, she took the palms of her hands and traced the water's path down his belly.

"My God," Cole whispered as he slowly turned to jelly.

Debbie sighed. Her dark eyes shadowed with barely disguised desire as she ran her fingernail lightly against the tan skin of his forearm. And then she pointed.

"Look," she urged.

His eyes followed the path her hands were taking. And when he saw her pointing to his arm, he got the message. He was solid goosebumps, and it had nothing to do with being cold. He was hot from the inside out.

"Those, my brilliant detective, are willies." Her fingertip was squarely atop a patch of goosebumps. "In fact, if I do say so myself, you've got a marvelous case of them."

Cole cleared his throat twice before he could speak. "So, Doc, if I've got them, what's my cure?"

The water's pull kept urging her back into depths over her head. He watched, fascinated as her slender body kept bobbing lightly up and down while she tried to maintain footing in the pool. Impulse sent his arms around her as he began moving them into deeper waters.

"Oh, Cole," Debbie teased, laughing and spitting water as he pushed her deeper and deeper into the pool until she was only afloat by holding onto his shoulders. "I'm afraid there's no cure."

He frowned. He could have told her that.

"But," she continued, enjoying their little game, "there's a very successful treatment." Her eyes were dancing by this time as she locked her arms around his neck and wrapped her legs around his waist to stay above water. "And you're in luck."

He grinned. "That's all a matter of opinion," he said. *I feel more like I'm in heat than in luck, lady. But I'm not admitting that to you...or anyone else.*

"I just happen to be an expert at administering doses."

"I'm a big man," Cole reminded her. "It'll take a big dose." By now, he knew what was coming. He could hardly wait.

"It would be my pleasure," Debbie whispered against his mouth.

Their lips merged, water slick, cool, and firm. Between them, their flesh warmed as they molded to each other's shape and savored the sensations of the kiss.

Her sigh became a moan and, as his arms tightened, became a groan. Cole dropped his hands instantly, remembering her injuries. But when he turned her loose, she started to sink. It only took a heartbeat to realize what he'd done.

"Lord have mercy," he muttered, dived beneath the water, and scooped her up before she touched bottom. Surfacing in moments, they both laughed and sputtered as water streamed from their hair into their eyes.

"If you didn't like the treatment, you should have just said so, not tried to drown me." Debbie laughed, as she wiped hair and water from her eyes.

Cole held her tight against his chest as he walked them both into shallow waters. "That's not the trouble, lady. I liked getting the damned condition nearly as much as the cure. I just don't think you're ready for the consequences."

It was one of the few times in her life that she was speechless. It gave her hope. It gave her courage. It

was the first time he'd ever openly admitted that there
was something between them he wanted to explore.

"That's where you're wrong, mister," she said. Her
voice was steady, her confidence sure. "I'll be ready
and waiting for the *consequences* long before you see
them coming."

He sighed and closed his eyes, for the moment just
relishing the feeling of holding her in his arms.

"Are you ready to come inside?" he asked, as he
finally set her back on even footing.

"No, I want to stay out awhile longer. But don't let
me stop you. If you're tired, go on to bed. I can take
care of myself."

He stared long and hard at the small woman with
the large bruises and even bigger determination
splashed across her face.

"I know you can," he said.

He walked over to the edge of the pool and pulled
himself up onto the side. Evening shadows shaded the
water. His legs dangled as he watched her swimming
back into deeper depths. "But maybe I *want* to help,
Deborah Jean."

She didn't hear him. She was too far away.

Chapter 7

Morgan hung up the phone and tried to mask his apprehension before he turned back to take his seat at the dinner table.

"Well, now there's more for me," he said jovially as he reclaimed his seat.

Debbie didn't miss a thing. She'd seen his hesitation. She'd heard the concern in his voice during the conversation. And she'd have to have been blind not to recognize that fake smile.

"What?" she asked.

"Something came up." Morgan shrugged, trying not to dwell on the possibilities occurring to him. Cole had been vague. He always was. But Morgan had heard the tension in his voice. He knew that whatever was "about to go down" was not the last bite of dessert Buddy was eyeing.

"Morgan Brownfield!"

The sharp tone of her voice got his attention.

Even Buddy quit dawdling. His spoon clattered onto the table and bounced onto the floor. He looked down at the spoon. He looked back up at Debbie. When he saw that she wasn't yelling at him, he retrieved his spoon from the floor, stuck it back in his ice cream, scooped, and ate, relieved that for once he was not the one in trouble.

Morgan was getting a first-hand glimpse of the woman who'd tied his son in knots. He started talking. He had no choice.

"I don't know details," he offered. "I never do. But something happened. I don't know whether it was a tip or new information or what. Anyway, as Cole put it, 'Something came up.' He doesn't know when he'll be home." Morgan watched the fear spreading on Debbie's face. "He'll be fine," he assured her. "This has happened lots of times before."

Debbie sat frozen in place. Every word Morgan was uttering was flashing images in her brain she didn't want to contemplate.

"His last orders were for us to take care of you," Morgan added.

Tears flashed. She hadn't even known they were coming. Her mouth twisted. She swallowed a lump of pain that tightened her throat and quietly arose from her chair.

"Well, then that's that," she said. "No need keeping stuff warm." She gathered her empty plate.

"Buddy, darling, when you're through, would you carry out the garbage?"

If she'd asked him to strip naked and then paint the garage, he couldn't have been more shocked. And then he caught his father's glare and swallowed the last bit of ice cream stuck on his tongue. It was a little large and a lot cold and made tears come as it hurt all the way down. But he quickly agreed. Something about the way she was standing so small and stiff with her back to the table told him that this was no time to be dense. And when he had to, Robert Allen Brownfield could be very astute. He took out the garbage.

Debbie was exhausted. The last forty-eight hours had been hell. To get past the worry of what might be happening to Cole, she'd cleaned every closet in sight, rearranged cabinets, and polished and repolished silverware and woodwork until Morgan had succumbed to her spree and disappeared to the golf course.

Buddy had locked his door in panic, certain that his precious room would be next in line. When night came on the second day, they'd all fallen into bed, relieved that the worst was over. They'd survived. There was nothing left to clean.

The night was muggy. Debbie lay uncovered, her silky yellow shift bunched around her thighs. She kept trying to find a comfortable position, but her clothes stuck to her body, and her hair wilted against her neck, making sleep impossible.

Knowing that Cole was not across the hall was a constant reminder that she didn't know where he was or what he was doing. She'd tried to ignore the fact that she was more than a little nervous about his safety. So she'd nearly killed herself by staying too busy to dwell on worries. And, it had almost worked. It was only when the house was dark and quiet, when everything was in place and all were asleep, that rest became impossible, though she was tired enough.

Maybe I'm too tired. I just need to relax.

She thought of the pool and the cool, calming water, and made a decision. It would be a quick dip. No need to change into her suit. Everyone else had been asleep hours ago. Her nighttime prowl couldn't possibly disturb them. Their rooms were at the opposite end of the house.

She grabbed a towel from her bathroom and padded down the hallway, a slip of yellow moving through the shadows.

The tall, wooden fence that surrounded the backyard protected property and privacy alike. It was enough. The night was dark and lonesome without the moon's presence. Streetlights from the front of the house stingily shed just enough light with which to maneuver.

The concrete was still warm, a reminder that the day had been hot. Her toes curled with anticipation as the water lapped quietly against the sides of the pool, moving gently in the rhythm of the night's feeble breeze. She stood beside a deck chair, inhaling the scents of a mimosa tree in full bloom and the bird of

paradise flowers opening to the **night**. The darkness
was familiar. She relaxed as it wrapped her in its shadows.

The straps of her gown disappeared with her tension. One slipped down and off and the other followed.
The yellow gown hung suspended on the thrust of her
breasts before she tugged. It fell at her feet, a puddle
of sunlight splattered on midnight. She walked to the
edge of the pool, lifted her arms above her head, and
leaned forward. Her fingertips parted the water, and
then it flowed over and around her, caressing her skin
like a wanton lover. She surfaced with a quiet laugh
and began to swim.

Cole stood in the shadows of the kitchen, moved
beyond words at the sight he beheld. He'd walked into
the house just as Debbie had walked out. His ears
caught the sound of the patio door catching, and instinctively, he went to investigate. He'd expected to
catch a thief. And in a manner of speaking, he had.
Debbie Randall had stolen his sanity weeks ago. Tonight she'd just stolen his heart.

His breath was tight within his chest. His lungs ex-
panded in shock as he watched her gown come off.
She offered herself to the night and the water, and he
resented the fact that it hadn't been to him. His feet
moved of their own accord as he walked out of the
house. Silently, he stood in the shadows and witnessed
the water covering her, caressing her. It was more than
a man could stand.

He bent down. His shoes came off. He straightened and began to undress. His jacket fell across the patio table, his gun and holster beneath it. Next came his shirt. His fingers paused at the button-fly of his jeans when something—an unbreakable code of honor—made him hesitate. No matter how much a rejection might hurt, he'd have to ask. He couldn't take. Not with her.

"Can anyone join in, or is this a private party?"

His deep, husky voice startled her. She stopped in midstroke and made a small, splashy U-turn in the pool. Her feet weren't touching, so she paddled until they did, swiped her hair from her face and the drops from her eyes, letting the water's turbulence lap at her breasts.

She stared, missing nothing of the fact that he was nearly undressed. She lifted her arm and motioned, a silent beckoning, then held her breath in wanton fascination as Cole stripped away the last of his clothing, leaving him bronzed and bare in the shadows of the night.

He was already hard and yearning. She tried not to stare at his body, but couldn't resist. He wanted, and it was because of her. It made her own body echo with an ache he could not see.

He stepped into the shallow end of the pool and walked toward her like a man in a trance. The water lapped at his knees and then his thighs. She started toward him, at first moving slowly against the thrust of the water and then faster as she moved toward the shallow end. And then they were face to face.

The water enveloped him. He was hot and hard, throbbing with desire, and knew there was no danger of losing that overwhelming feeling. Not when his lady was coming toward him wearing nothing but diamond droplets of H_2O. They ran in pearlized perfection down her body, illuminated by the faint lights that penetrated the shrubs and trees surrounding the backyard.

The water rested at the boundary just below his navel. Debbie stopped, suddenly a bit wary, a bit afraid of what she'd unleashed with her invitation. This man wore many faces. But the face of a lover was one with which she was not yet familiar. Her breath caught in the back of her throat as his hand reached out and caressed the nearly faded bruise on her shoulder.

"I'm afraid I'll hurt you." His voice was harsh and needy.

Debbie lifted her arms. "Only if you stop."

With a groan, he caught her up, lifting her high, nearly out of the water, and then let her down, sliding her cool, wet body against him, and tried not to shake from the emotions that overwhelmed him.

She was tiny, but so perfect. Her breasts cushioned against his chest as his hands spanned her waist. The curvaceous flare of her hips fit his ache as she wrapped her legs around his middle and let him walk them both into deeper waters.

And then her mouth tilted and caught his next moan, slipping across his lips with wet precision.

"I've never wanted or needed anyone in my life the way I want you, lady."

Cole's voice was harsh and aching. His hands slid around her, tracing the path of her spine as the water enveloped them. Cupping her hips, he let the water rock her against him. He shuddered, wanting to thrust now. Needing to disappear into the woman beneath him. And yet he waited.

Debbie was lost beneath the spell of the night and the man above her. His hands did things of which she'd never dreamed. His mouth wove magic into the act of love. She needed to belong to him wholly, to take the man inside her and feel his heat and his strength. But he resisted the final motion that would complete the thought. Instead, he continued to investigate her body with a mind-bending thoroughness.

"Come here, sweetheart," Cole whispered. He walked them both toward the side of the pool.

Debbie's head touched the edge, and instinctively, her hands went backwards and grasped the sides to keep her from sinking. She knew she was in over her head...in more ways than one. She was helpless at the hands of this man.

Her body arched, parting the water as she anchored herself to the side of the pool. The movement thrust her breasts up and out, enticing and taunting, and Cole could not resist. His mouth swooped and he encircled the tight little bud at the center of one breast, relishing the hard throb of her pulse beneath his tongue. He rolled it gently between his teeth and felt her body buck beneath him as the tiny pain sent shafts of pleasure throughout her system. He laughed once, low and distinct, and then drank from the droplets in the shadowy valley between her breasts as he journeyed across to the other side and took similar license.

His heart pounded. His manhood throbbed. The water was nothing but a silken torture, lapping and teasing with ever-constant movement. His hands slid down below the surface and between her thighs, parting them with gentle persuasion as she opened to receive him.

He might have been able to wait. It just might have been possible to prolong the delicious torture of fluid foreplay, but she moved. And he slid too close to the heat and fell into the pleasure.

For one long moment, neither moved. But their shock at the joining was fleeting as their need grew.

Her grip tightened on the side of the pool as Cole entered her more deeply. Letting her float free, his hands encircled her waist and he began to move.

She moaned once, the size of him more than she'd imagined, yet no more than she could stand. He was hot and hard and silken, a motion of magic inside her body.

Her groan made him panic. "Am I hurting you, baby?" he whispered, uncertain how he'd ever be able to withdraw from the sweetness.

"Not enough…not enough."

Her answer drove him over the edge. Cole caught his breath at the magnitude of feelings that over-whelmed him. For the first time in his life, he was home…and he knew it…and it scared him to death. But he'd needed too much and had stepped over the line.

The water rocked her gently, and then Cole gripped her waist and rocked her again. Slowly at first and then with increasing speed and depth, he took her right to the edge.

Her eyes were closed as she drifted, lost inside her-self at the emotions swamping her. Cole gritted his teeth, felt himself losing control, and made one last effort to prolong the ecstasy.

"Lady…"

His agonized whisper brought her back in an in-stant. She looked up into a black passion and tried to smile. But the feelings were too strong, and she turned loose of the pool and grabbed onto him as he took them down.

She burst from the inside out. Bubbles of pleasure shot out in jet strength to every nerve ending and then drifted lazily throughout her limbs, making her bone-weak and unable to stand.

Cole felt himself die as he emptied inside her. Sink-ing and sighing, shuddering with a surfeit of passion, he held her tight and took them back to the top with his last ounce of strength.

They burst through the surface, taking in air, holding onto each other, because alone, neither of them would have been strong enough to stand.

They stared long and hard into each other's eyes while their breathing returned to normal and sanity regained its rightful place in their world. But nothing would ever again be the same. They'd crossed over a boundary into uncharted waters. Cole watched the slow smile spreading on her face.

"What?" he asked gently as he bent down and tasted the smile. It was warmer than he'd expected. He smoothed hair and water from her eyes and blessed the corner of her lips with a kiss.

Debbie returned the favor, drinking from the droplets that lingered on his mouth. Letting her tongue rasp over the beard-roughened jaw clenching at her touch. She was tasting and savoring the texture of her man.

"You know what this means, don't you?" she asked.

His arms tightened around her. His body was already reminding him that he'd only gotten a taste of what he still hungered for.

"I know what this means to me," he growled. "I've marked you, woman. You may not see it, and you may not be able to feel it, but you've just been branded as thoroughly as those calves were at the Longren Ranch."

"You're wrong," Debbie whispered as her hands slid down his body and encompassed that which was already changing again. "I can see and feel just fine."

She taunted him mercilessly with a gentle upward thrust. "But there's something you haven't realized."

"What?" he moaned as her hands slid up and down the growing length of him. He was desperately trying to concentrate on her words when all he wanted was to concentrate on the mass of feelings she was erecting inside him.

"I won't let you go, Cole Brownfield. Not now. Not ever again. You made the decision for both of us tonight. You belong to me, just as surely as I belong to you."

God help us! Then all prayer was lost as Cole swept her from the water before she drowned them both. Somehow they made it to his room, clothes in hand. He dropped his gun in a drawer and their clothes on the floor. He couldn't think past the woman on his bed and the fever in his brain.

He headed toward the kitchen, following the sound of voices. His shower-damp hair was nearly black against his neck as tiny droplets of water he'd forgotten to dry ran in neat little paths down his clean, dry T-shirt. Long legs wearing denim made giant strides toward her voice. He tried to mask the burst of pleasure that shot through him when he walked into the room. Then gave it up as a lost cause when she turned, spatula in one hand, platter of pancakes in the other, and smiled.

Morgan glanced up from the article he'd been reading in the morning paper.

"Morning, son," he muttered, and started to resume his reading when the look on Cole's face registered. He crumpled the paper in his lap and stared.

Buddy was sopping the last of his pancakes through a pool of syrup. He spoke around the bite.

"Hi, Cole." He chewed.

Cole walked past them, took the plate and spatula out of Debbie's hands, and wrapped her arms around his waist.

"Good morning, lady," he whispered against her ear. "I thought I'd lost you." He was referring to the fact that he'd awakened alone.

"Fat chance." She grinned and turned her face up for the kiss she saw coming.

Morgan gaped. Buddy dropped his fork. Syrup splattered onto his shirt, the table, and the butter dish. He stared openmouthed and then grinned. As if to celebrate what he saw, he swiped his fingers across a droplet of syrup and then licked his finger shiny clean before going on to the next splash.

Morgan rolled his eyes and then tried to glare at the fact that he had a grown son who was licking syrup off the table.

"Mother always said, 'Waste not, want not.' Remember?" Buddy remarked.

"She also said you were a pig," Cole reminded him as he reluctantly turned Debbie loose.

"How many do you want?" she asked, indicating the remaining pancake batter waiting for her to turn it into golden orbs with crisp, lacy edges.

"How many can you spare?" he teased, and bent down and stole one more kiss before she shooed him to the table with her spatula.

"Well!" Morgan finally managed to say. "It's amazing what a good night's sleep will do for a man."

Cole grinned but declined to comment. Debbie blushed lightly, but kept her chin tilted at a proud, nearly defiant angle. There was no shame in her heart. Only joy.

Cole managed to eat without making a total fool of himself. He neatly dodged Buddy's attempt to tease him and ignored his father's prodding comments. *Thank God for years of police work and this poker face,* he thought.

The phone rang. To save himself the indignity of ignoring his father's last question regarding his intentions and Debbie's good name, he jumped up and answered it before its second ring.

"Case! Hi, man!" And then Cole grinned broadly. "Is this call what I think it is?" He whooped. "That's great! They're all right here. Wait a minute. I'll put Dad on."

"Grandpa, it's for you."

Morgan let out an echoing whoop as he hurried to answer the phone. "Hi, Case," he yelled. "Oh sorry, guess I was a little loud. I'm just excited. A man doesn't become a grandfather every day. What do we have? A boy or a girl?"

He turned and mouthed to the trio behind him. *It's a boy!*

Buddy celebrated by swiping one last droplet of syrup and rushed to take his turn at the phone. He thought he just might like being an uncle, especially since it would be a long-distance relationship that would not require changing diapers and the like.

"Lily had a baby!" Cole grinned as he turned to Debbie.

And then the smile slipped off his face to be replaced with instant shock. He'd just remembered last night...and the pool.

"My God!" He shook.

"What's wrong?" she asked. His behavior was more than strange. "Nothing's wrong with Lily or the baby? Please, Cole, tell me what's—"

"Last night. I didn't...we should have..."

Relief washed over her. "It's all right," she said, instantly cognizant of his panic. Her voice was barely past a whisper as she caught his face in her hands and pulled him down to her level. "I'm protected. You won't be caught in that trap, mister, not by me." Her tone of voice was almost bitter and full of sarcasm.

He pulled back and threaded his fingers through her hair, holding her in place as his harsh whisper made her blush with shame. "A child—our child—wouldn't be a trap, lady. And I was only thinking of you. Not me."

She shrugged and blinked back tears. "I didn't mean that the way it sounded, Cole. I guess that's an old brand I've carried a bit too long."

He frowned as the tears sparkled behind her gaze. "I don't understand, honey."

"I know you don't," she said. "But while I was growing up, every time my parents had a fight, my existence became a major issue. I was probably about twelve before it dawned on me that I came along before their wedding."

"Well, hell," Cole muttered, and pulled her against him, pressing her face against his heartbeat. It made him hurt to think of Debbie trying to live down someone else's shame. "It's no big deal, you know. I wish they were still alive, girl. I'd like to thank them for putting the cart before the horse, so to speak. I'd hate to think of my world without you in it."

She tried to smile past the tears but never made it. They spilled over and ran silently down her face.

"What's wrong with Debbie?" Morgan asked. He'd relinquished the phone to Buddy and then suddenly became aware of the fact that everyone else wasn't shouting for joy.

Cole answered without looking up. "You know how women are, Dad. She's just happy."

Morgan wrapped them both in his arms. "It's been so long since we've had a woman on the place, I'd forgotten that little trick." He grinned and hugged them tightly. "From the greeting you two gave each other this morning, it looks like I'm about to get a refresher course on it. All I can say is this has been one of the happiest days of my life. I got a grandson and another daughter handed to me."

Cole's eyebrows rose. His smile was lopsided as he stared his father straight in the face and tried not to sound too sarcastic as he said, "Well, Dad, it looks like you have everything all figured out. When you get the details in place, let Debbie and me know what's happening."

Debbie kicked Cole lightly in the shins and then ignored his gasp of pain.

"What did they name the baby?" she asked.

She knew that, with Cole, commitment did not automatically follow the act of love. That he felt deeply for her was an obvious given. He might even love her. But he'd said nothing to her. And when she heard it, it must be from his lips first. She didn't want his father pressuring him into something he wasn't ready to face.

"Oh! Right! A name! Buddy, give me the phone. I forgot to ask."

Morgan made a dive for the phone and relegated Buddy to the sidelines again.

"I'm sorry," Cole said.

"I'm not," she whispered. "Not about one single, solitary thing that's happened between us. Not from the first day I arrived. And not about last night, either. Just because your father assumed something doesn't put you on the spot with me, Cole Brownfield. What happened last night doesn't either. You have to want me as much as I want you, and then we'll talk. Until then, why don't you just go with the flow, darlin'. You California people live life too fast. You need to take it one day at a time." Then she leaned forward and whispered against his lips, "Nice and easy…it's the only way to go."

He grinned and closed his eyes as he tasted her words. They were reminiscent of last night's loving and this morning's breakfast. It was the first time he'd ever realized that making love and maple syrup were alike—both of them slow moving and very, very sweet. And then she walked out of his arms and up to the phone.

"My turn." She smiled as Morgan handed her the phone and a kiss.

Cole watched the expressions coming and going on her face and knew that he was over his head in love with Deborah Randall. What he did about it would be an entirely different matter. For one long, delicious moment he allowed himself to dream—about loving and life and Debbie and babies. And then he saw a familiar brown leather wallet lying on the counter. He walked over and picked it up.

His badge.

He knew instantly when he'd lost it. Last night, when he'd shed every stitch of both clothing and inhibition and crawled into the pool with her.

His fingers traced the outline of his badge, smoothing the cool metal until it warmed beneath his touch. Worry tinged the edges of his conscience, but he shoved it back into a deeper part of his mind. Today was not a day for borrowing troubles. Today was not the day to decide if his life and a wife would coincide. His baby sister was now a mother. It was enough…just for today.

Chapter 8

Thomas Holliday was pissed. He looked at his reflection as he walked past a store window and frowned. He had a deep scratch on his face and two more on his neck.

Damn fool bitch!

Last night Nita Warren had given him some cock-and-bull excuse about not wanting to make it because he wouldn't wear a condom. He'd tried every excuse and plea he could think of and then when she'd persisted, he's slapped her around and done it anyway. He didn't know why she'd cried and argued. Women were all alike. They didn't know what they wanted. But he did. They wanted someone to take control and show them a good time. He was real good at taking control. And he could care less if they had a good time. It was his own pleasure that mattered most.

A police car turned the corner in front of him, and for one moment, his heart accelerated and jumped into the roof of his mouth. He swallowed it back where it belonged, took a deep breath, and stared at the cruiser's taillights as it went past.

He didn't know why he was so jumpy. But he kept remembering that woman from the beach. It was more than a coincidence that she'd seen him make the snatch, and then saw him again at the mall. It had never happened before. He'd never left witnesses...at least, none that were willing to talk.

He shook off his nervousness. It was only snatch and grab. He didn't know why he was worrying. Cops had bigger fish to fry. He hitched at the bulge behind his zipper and strutted off down the street.

Jackie Warren wiped at his nose with the back of his hand. His sister, Nita, had come home crying last night, claiming that she'd been raped. He'd tried to work up a rage of family loyalty but it had been lost in his need for a fix. Granted he was the man of the family now that his old man was in the joint, but today wasn't a good day for Jackie. At least, it hadn't been until he'd made the rounds. He'd heard on the streets that the cops were looking for Thomas Holliday. It had worked up his weak need for justice and revenge all over again, especially since he knew that he could sell his information and replenish his supply in one fell swoop. Ordinarily, one street-wise tough didn't sell out another. But Jackie Warren held a distinct but little known title. He was what was known as a "source." He sold information to the cops and, in return, kept his nose in business. Jackie Warren headed for the phone. He had an instantaneous need to unburden his soul.

"Don't fix dinner tonight," Cole said, as he started out the door. "We're invited to Rick and Tina's."

"Cole..." His name was a gentle reminder on her lips that he'd told her, not asked. It was also a re- minder that he was about to leave without telling her goodbye.

He made it outside before he stopped and turned around, walked back inside the house, and hauled her off her feet and into his arms.

"Lady, you're the only person I've ever known who could draw my name out into more than one syllable."

"You don't like it?"

He nuzzled the side of her neck and traced the inner shell of her ear with his tongue. "It's the sexiest thing I've ever heard," he whispered.

"Good," she answered. "I have nothing against sex." She ignored his laugh. "And now, what was it you were muttering about as you were so rudely leav- ing?"

"Rick wants us to come over. Tina's been dying to meet you. Are you up to it? Don't feel obligated to come on—"

Debbie's hands slid around his back as her whisper slid across his mouth. "I'm *up* to just about anything that you're *up* to. And I'd love to meet your friends. Tell them we're coming. Morgan and Buddy can eat pizza.''

Cole shivered. Her sexy references to being "up" had nothing to do with dinner invitations, and they both knew it. His body ached. It had been too long since he'd shared her bed. Cohabitating in a house with too many people had its drawbacks. Basically, it just couldn't be done without openly admitting it was happening. And, he couldn't bring himself to ignore her feelings. He didn't want her embarrassed in front of his family. But he wanted her. And they both knew it.

"Be ready about six." He kissed her once as he started to leave and then turned. The look he gave her was more than a promise of promptness. It was full of assurances that he would come back. And he would be safe. "I won't be late." And then he was gone.

Debbie wiggled. She wrapped her arms around herself and tried not to smile. But it was no use. Buddy was the first to benefit from her joy. He walked into the living room and stopped, caught in place by the look on her face.

"Uh…" He didn't know whether to run or stand and take it. She didn't give him a choice. She threw herself into his arms and announced, "I love you, Robert Allen Brownfield. In fact, I love all the Brownfields. And just because I do, I'm going to make you a cherry pie."

Morgan walked in on the scene and began to grin.

He'd heard Cole leaving. He knew what had put that smile on Debbie's face.

"What about me?" Morgan teased. "I'm a poor old grandfather without sustenance…or sense. If I had any, I'd have dumped these fool sons of mine years ago and found myself someone like you."

"Pooh," Debbie said. "But you'll share the pie, won't you, Buddy?"

His attention wavered. He'd just gotten used to the idea of pie. He wasn't certain about the sharing part at all.

"Can't you, Buddy?" Debbie was persistent.

He caved in. "Lily named her baby, Charles Morgan Longren. I think I'll call him Charlie."

Debbie and Morgan stared at each other, trying to make sense of what Buddy had just said. They knew the baby had been named for both grandfathers. What it had to do with cherry pies was beyond either of them.

"That's a good idea, son," Morgan said as Buddy wandered away. And then he turned and fixed Debbie with a hard, warning look. "If you and Cole have a child like Buddy, I may disown the both of you."

She blushed. First at the thought of having Cole's child, and then at the thought that Morgan knew it might be possible. That meant he knew, or suspected, what had happened between them.

"Don't," Morgan said, instantly sorry for what he'd inadvertently implied. "I'm sorry. I'm just an old man meddling into other people's—"

"You're not old, and you don't meddle." She laughed. "And I've got to go make a pie."

She disappeared into the kitchen. Morgan saw the shadows in her eyes. He knew she masked her apprehension behind teasing and laughter. And he suspected that his son was dragging his feet about commitments. He sighed. *I'm too old for this nonsense,* he thought. *And Cole is a bigger fool than I'd ever imagined if he lets this one get away.*

A smaller version of Rick Garza met them at the door wearing the latest in Batman gear and sporting a Superman cape. Debbie smiled. This kid was hedging his bets. If one superhero failed him, he had another on which to fall back.

"Hi, Uncle Cole. Who's that?" He pointed at Debbie and blew a bubble that popped across his nose and chin.

"That's my girl," Cole answered, and grinned as the small child made a gagging noise and fell to the floor in an exaggerated fit of disgust.

"Yuck," Enrique said, his dark eyes flashing with merriment. He heard his mother coming and rolled to his feet as she came dashing into the room.

"Enrique! Your manners." Rick's wife, Tina, made a flying leap for her child and frowned as he ducked her grab and swooped away down the hall shrieking the theme from Batman.

"I'm sorry," Tina Garza said. "Seven is a difficult age." And then she grinned. "Six wasn't any better and neither was five or..." she shrugged. "You get the picture. Come in. You must be Debbie."

Debbie nodded and walked into a house warm with laughter and love, smothered in jalapeños and cheeses. The aroma of something delicious and Mexican drifted across her path.

She'd already met Rick. Her trip to the emergency room was one she'd like to forget, but not the driver. Rick had been as concerned for her welfare as had Cole. He'd pushed the limits of street safety to get her to the hospital as fast a possible.

The relaxed atmosphere at the Garzas' home was a welcome respite from the busy traffic of Laguna Beach. She took a deep breath and had the most insane urge to kick off her shoes and follow Tina Garza into the kitchen. She felt welcome.

Cole visibly unwound. It was obvious that this was his home away from home.

"Hey, you guys!" Rick yelled from the adjoining room. "You're just in time. The hundred-meter free-style is about to begin. Come on in." He was glued to the set, watching the prerecorded telecasts of the day's Olympic events.

Tina rolled her eyes. "Come with me," she urged, taking Debbie by the hand. "You can help chop tomatoes. Those two aren't worth two pesos when there's a sporting event on television."

Cole disappeared with a shrug and a grin, and Debbie followed Tina into the kitchen, missing nothing of her diminutive height or the slightly rounded belly that gave away the fact that little Batman Garza was about to lose his standing in the family as "an only child."

Tina handed her a bowl of tomatoes and a paring knife.

Debbie began to peel and dice according to her hostess's instructions.

"When are you due?" Debbie's voice was wistful.

Tina rubbed her stomach, and her dark eyes softened perceptibly as her mouth curved upward. "I'm only five months. I have a way to go. But we're hoping for a girl."

"Cole's sister just had a baby boy," Debbie said. "Did you know Lily?"

"Only by name," Tina said. "She'd already moved out of the house when Cole and Rick became partners."

Tina saw the look in Debbie's eyes every time Cole's name was mentioned. All the worries she'd had regarding this woman from Oklahoma who'd captured Cole's heart just disappeared. It was obvious that Debbie was very much in love with the man. She couldn't understand what was holding them back from making an announcement about their relationship.

"So, have you known Cole long?" Tina asked.

"In here—" Debbie touched her heart "—all my life. It just took me a long time to find him."

Tina caught her breath at the lyrical way Debbie described falling in love.

"Then what's he going to do about it?"

The shocked look on Debbie's face had Tina smiling apologetically. "I guess you see where Enrique gets his rudeness. Rick says I have no tact. But I care for Cole and I want him to be happy."

Debbie's hands stilled. Shadows darkened her eyes. "I don't know what he's going to do," she said softly. "I'm just waiting."

"I don't understand," Tina said.

"Sometimes I don't either," Debbie said. "But I think it has something to do with his being a policeman...and not getting married. What do you think?"

Tina threw her hands into the air and let loose with a string of Spanish. Debbie sat on the bar stool, stunned by Tina's volatile outbreak as tomato juice ran down her elbows and onto the floor.

"You're leaking," Rick said, as he swiped a paper towel across Debbie's arms and then down onto the floor. "And we can hear you in the other room, *chiquita.*" He leaned down and softened his criticism with a kiss.

Debbie looked down in surprise at the juice on her arms and jumped up, hoping that none of it had gotten on her clothing. She breathed a quick sigh of relief. She'd been spared.

"Now that you've cursed the four corners of the earth, my love, when can we expect our food?"

Tina made a playful swipe in Rick's direction and shoved him away. "Get out of my kitchen. You eat when we're through and not another minute before." Then as he tried to make a graceful exit, she called after him, "Pour yourselves a little tequila. Soften up that fool you call a partner. Maybe my spicy cooking and this pretty woman will make him come to his senses.''

Rick's eyebrows arched. His mouth pursed and a knowing expression came on his face. "Now, I know what set you off. You know what I've told you. Matchmaking doesn't become you. Just let well enough alone, okay?''

Tina ignored him. "We eat in a few minutes. Go back to your Olympic games.''

Debbie smiled at the interchange between the pair. It was obvious from the way Rick touched Tina's cheek and then her belly before he left that the love between them was strong. *If only Cole could see, if only he'd let himself realize that marriages can work…and do.*

The meal was finally served. And if Debbie thought the first bite was hot, she was totally convinced by the last one that Tina Garza had no spices left in her kitchen. She'd obviously used them all in her cooking.

"It was too hot?" Tina's dark eyes mirrored concern as Debbie downed another glass of water.

"I'm not sure." Debbie grinned. "But I think it took all the hair off my tongue.''

Enrique looked up from his meal and, for the first time since their arrival, took notice of the woman with his Uncle Cole. "You have hair on your tongue?" he asked with interest, and ran his finger across his own, testing the surface.

Laughter erupted. "It's just an expression, Son," Rick said. "I think it is probably a special one that only people in Oklahoma use."

"Oh no," Debbie assured him. "My grandmother always said that, and she was from Tennessee." Then she lowered her voice and leaned over until she was eye level with Rick's young son. "And, she also said that eating tomatoes sprinkled with black pepper made hair grow on a man's chest."

Enrique looked with interest at the bowl of pico de gallo that he'd refused all night long. He stared at Debbie and then back at the bowl and nodded sagely as if instantly understanding the logic of such a statement. And when he thought no one was looking, dished himself up a serving of the chopped tomato and onion, sprinkled it liberally with black pepper, and took it like a dose of medicine.

Cole tried not to laugh. But the intensity with which the child was chewing was too much. And when Enrique subversively slid his little hand up beneath the front of his Batman shirt and rubbed his chest, testing to see if anything had sprouted, it was too much to ignore.

"You have just moved up a notch in my book," Tina said. "I've been trying to get him to eat tomatoes for a year."

Debbie looked up and grinned. "It always worked on my younger brother, Douglas. I see that it hasn't lost its magic." Calmly, she mumbled an aside to

Cole. "I wonder what would happen if I sprinkled you with pepper?"

Rick whooped at the look of panic on Cole's face. "Man alive, you didn't exaggerate about her, did you, buddy?"

Tina fairly bubbled with glee.

"I guess it all depends where you sprinkle," Cole mumbled, and then joined in the laughter.

"We're home," Cole said, and gently patted Debbie's shoulder.

She'd dozed off less than five minutes after leaving the Garza residence, and Cole had taken the long way home just to give himself the pleasure of watching her sleep.

The word *home* sank into her sleepy consciousness. It sounded so wonderful. If it were only true. She stretched, moaned, and started to crawl out of the car.

Cole met her at the door and slid his arm around her shoulders. Together, they walked into the house and then caught their breath at the quiet...and the note propped against the salt and pepper shakers on the kitchen table.

> Thanks for the pie. Buddy and I went to a movie. We'll be *very* late coming home. Have a good evening.
>
> Love, Morgan

"We've been set up," Debbie said, handing Cole the note.

"First Tina, now Dad. It looks like I'd get the message, doesn't it?" Cole's smile was forced.

"Oh, you already got the message," Debbie drawled. "You're just dragging your feet. And, you'd better pick 'em up, cause where I come from, sometimes you come away with more than dirt on them."

She walked off, leaving Cole alone in the middle of the room with a shocked expression plastered across his face.

She was almost to her room when her feet left the floor. Arms snaked around her waist and lifted her up and against a heartbeat out of control.

"Cole! You scared me to death." Her words were sharp, but came out gentle and easy.

"No, lady," he said, pressing her hand against his chest. "This is what scared feels like. But right now, it would feel worse if I let you go. Do you understand?"

She heard what was between the lines of his confession. "I understand, Cole Brownfield. Now, take me to bed, and damn tomorrow. The only thing that matters is what's between us tonight."

There were many things in a man's lifetime that he might regret. But for Cole, loving this woman would never be one of them. He stared at the faint light coming through his curtains and smiled softly to himself as Debbie shifted against his side, nestling herself against him.

If he could only find the nerve to tell her what she

meant to him. If he could just trust the fact that she loved him enough to stay and to give him the space to do what he must. Being a cop was all he'd ever wanted. He couldn't—and wouldn't—give it up. Not for anyone. But finding that someone special who was willing and able to share him with his job had seemed impossible. Until now.

An overwhelming need to reclaim her made him shake. It had been less than an hour since they'd made love with a desperation that left them both weak and weary. Now, just the knowledge that she was still here beside him made him hard all over again.

Debbie felt the rhythm of his breathing change. She slid her cheek against his rib cage and felt the rapidity of his heartbeat. Her breasts were lush and soft against him, emphasizing all the more the very special differences between this hard man with a gentle heart and the soft woman with determination made of steel. She'd found her man. She'd do what it took to keep him.

"Lady, I need you…again."

His voice rasped across her senses, making her shiver with anticipation at the delight which he was capable of giving.

"Then take, Cole Brownfield. It's yours. I'm yours."

He rolled over her, coming to a halt just inches above the tilt of breast teasing at his arrival. His body was hard and straining toward home. But this time, there would be no mutual sharing. This time, he needed to give. There would be a time for taking later.

His mouth descended, but skipped her lips and slid down past her chin, taking her breath with him. His hands moved, almost of their own accord, across her body and down the slender shape of her until they came to the parting of her thighs. They stilled, and so did her heart.

"For me, lady. Let this happen for me."

She sighed, dug her hands into his hair, and knew that she'd never be able to deny him.

"I'll do anything for you, Cole."

He groaned—a quiet sigh of desperate need that feathered across her belly. His mouth slid down across the tops of her thighs and sampled the texture, then paused. His breath on her skin was a warning of where he was about to go.

Debbie's eyes flew open in shock and then fell shut, heavy with passion, as Cole moved into unexplored territory with his mouth and hands. She gasped. And then conscious thought disappeared.

Nothing existed outside the man...and his mouth...and what he was doing with his hands. It was all she could do just to focus on breathing. Everything he did seemed to make it stop. Every stroke of his tongue sent shockwaves of sensation rocketing through her, and every caress of his hands turned her body to liquid fire.

Cole felt the impending rush building beneath his

touch. Every gasp, every moan she uttered made him crazy with need to be inside her when this happened.

But there was also the need to give without reservation to this woman. She'd already given so much and asked nothing in return. He knew what she wanted, but the only thing he was capable of giving her now, at this moment, was joy. A future was uncertain. He chose to live for the moment.

Sweet heat burst in his hands. He shuddered, feeling her passion as surely as if it were his own. And then it was. Cole moved upward, captured her gasps of pleasure and tasted her cry as release spiraled within her.

"Love you, love you," she whispered against his cheek.

Ah, Deborah Jean, I love you, too. But his thought was never voiced as Cole moved between her legs and settled himself into the heat. A single thrust ended his last sane thought. After that, he could remember nothing save the feel of her legs around him, her hands on his body, and her tears on his face as he took them back into the fire.

"Good morning…California!" the disc jockey cried as Cole's clock radio came on with maddening precision. "It's six a.m. and another day awaits. Here's a slow and easy wake-up call from Miss Bonnie Raitt with her latest hot single. Like the lady says, 'I can't make you love me, if you don't.'"

Deep and husky, the singer's voice wove a plaintive

message that made Debbie wish she'd slept through the alarm. *Oh, Cole. Not even my love can make your heart feel something it won't.*

Cole groaned and buried his face in the curve of her neck, unwilling to move or to tear himself loose of his lady. He dozed, unaware that Debbie was already lost in a world of hurt and despair.

Last night had been magic. But it was morning. And Debbie had waited all through the night for a word from this man that would make her world right. She'd been given pleasure. She'd been given joy. But the one thing she'd waited to hear was never spoken. He'd made love to her with deliberate and passionate skill. But he'd never said the words she needed to hear. He wouldn't say, I love you.

The phone rang, jarring the moment, and Cole muttered beneath his breath as he rolled over on his back, taking Debbie with him. He grabbed the receiver before the second ring.

"This better be good," he growled. And then his arms unconsciously tightened their hold on Debbie as he listened. And finally he spoke. "I'll be right there."

Debbie rolled over and out of bed, ignoring her nudity. "It seems I have no clothes," she said, masking her pain with a teasing sarcasm.

"Debbie!" Cole's voice was sharp. But his touch was gentle as she turned back to face him. "Don't shut me out, sweetheart," he begged. "Every time we get close, my job interferes, and then this wall comes up between us."

Debbie smiled through tears. "Is that how it seems?" She shrugged into his shirt, using it for a cover-up, and pulled away from his grasp. "I didn't know." Her voice was shaky, but her meaning was clear. "I didn't know we'd even been close."

She halted his stunned argument with a wave of her hand. "Oh, I know we've been close…bodily." The tears were thick behind her lashes. "But close? As in, heart-to-heart forever-love kind of close—no way, mister. You're the one who refuses to face facts. You're the one who shuts off whenever your job enters the picture. It's not me who's running. It's you."

She walked out of his room. The door shut with a quiet click, and Cole was left to absorb the truth of her accusations. He wanted to shout. He needed to argue…to fling her words back in her face. But he could do nothing in the face of truth.

Debbie slipped into her room and closed the door. She leaned back, letting the tears run. She tried to laugh away her foolishness, but there was nothing behind her lips but a sob. She'd known what she was getting into when she'd promised Lily she'd come. Only a fool would have ignored the warning signs that Cole Brownfield had left behind him when he'd run from Oklahoma.

But, love makes fools of us all, she thought. "Okay, mister. We've played dodge ball of the heart long enough. I give myself two more weeks, and then it's time to pack it in. If you can't see what you'll be throwing away, then I guess *I* was the blind one, after all.''

Her muttered vow was harsh. But no one heard. And in the end, it wouldn't have mattered if they had.

Cole was showered and dressed and in the kitchen, downing one quick cup of coffee when she walked into the room.

For one long moment, they stared at each other. He missed nothing of her still-wet lashes clinging together above eyes dark with pain, nor of the way her arms were folded across her chest—body language that told him he'd hurt her, and she was not open for more of the same.

She tugged at the oversized T-shirt skimming the hem of her shorts, and knew that she'd never be able to let him leave with this hurt between them. She sighed. It served her right for falling in love with principles, no matter how misguided.

"I suppose you think you're going to get a goodbye kiss?" she muttered.

The heavy band around his heart loosened just enough for him to answer. "I'd given it a little thought," he whispered, and then she was in his arms.

"You think too much," she said.

The kiss was bittersweet. The pain was still there. But a promise of something better came in the touching, and Cole left with the taste of her on his lips.

Chapter 9

Thomas Holliday got careless. He was broke, and it *had* been a week since the incident at the mall. It was time to get back on to the streets and do a little hustling. His fingers itched. His adrenaline raced. He swaggered down the steps of a friend's apartment. It was his residence for the week. Next week it would be somewhere else. Where he slept was the least of his worries.

It never occurred to him that he could work for money. That required too much effort and the payoff was, in his estimation, unworthy. It also never occurred to him that he made less as a thief than he would have working for minimum wages in a fast-food restaurant. Thomas Holliday wasn't known for his brains, only his fast hands and quick feet.

"Is that him?" The unmarked police car was parked about half a block away. The driver pointed as his partner grabbed a pair of binoculars and looked. He nodded, the mug shot that lay in the seat between them, a second verification of their prey.

"That's him," he said. "Hell, this is going to be too easy. He's even coming this way."

Thomas Holliday had just decided that he was going to have pancakes and sausage for ninety-nine cents at the drive-in on the corner. But the man getting out of the white car in front of him changed his mind. Holliday had a sneaking suspicion that his food was about to be compliments of the county for some time to come.

"Thomas Holliday, you're under arrest. You have the right to remain silent. If you—"

"I've heard it all before," he snarled.

But it didn't stop the officer as he read him his rights. Holliday cursed long and loud as he was handcuffed, placed in the back seat of the car, and driven away. Several blocks later, they turned a corner, and he saw the drive-in. The breakfast special was off. He should have known. This just wasn't his day. His stomach growled in protest as they continued down the street.

"Cole! Man, I didn't think you'd ever get here," Rick said.

Cole dropped into the chair behind his desk and

frowned as the coffee in his cup sloshed over the side and onto some papers.

"Here," Rick said. "I'll blot, you swallow. You're going to need all the control you can muster. Suck that caffeine, buddy."

"What's the big deal?" Cole muttered, as he dabbed at the spilled coffee with a paper towel Rick handed him.

"They pulled him in early this morning."

"Pulled who?" Cole's mind was still on Debbie. But it didn't take him long to get in gear as Rick answered.

"Thomas Holliday. A couple of Laguna Beach's finest picked him up this morning coming out of an apartment. They're talking to him now. It seems the little man has decided that he wants to make a deal. He keeps claiming that his purse snatching is small potatoes to the information he could give us regarding some dealers. He wants to walk for the information."

The coffee cup hit the desk empty. The look on Cole's face was blacker than the liquid he'd just consumed.

"Dammit to hell! No deals! Not with that son-of-a—"

"I knew you'd feel like that. So, come on, we've got some tall talking to do with the boys down in Theft."

"Detective Brownfield...Garza..."

The lieutenant in charge shook their hands as they

walked into his office. He knew both men well. The talk had spread quickly throughout the department that Cole Brownfield had a vested interest in this subject's arrest. It was a matter of courtesy to hear him out. And the information the perp was trying to sell to the cops came under Narcotics' jurisdiction. That *was* Cole's territory. It stood to reason that he and his partner would be called in.

"What has he said? What have you promised?" Cole's anger was obvious and barely contained.

Lieutenant Tanaka frowned. "He's said plenty. We're trying to decide what's valid and what's not. But it seems he's saving the "big stuff," as he calls it, for bigger guns, like you boys. He claims to have some inside info on the dealers around the warehouse district."

Cole's heart sank. He knew a petty thief's crimes would fall short of important in the light of something as big as putting a major dealer out of business.

"And we haven't promised him a damn thing." The lieutenant's voice was gruff. "My daughter was raped seven years ago. The bastard never even made it to trial. His lawyer made a deal." Venom poured from the lieutenant's words.

Cole understood. He could still close his eyes and see the shock on Debbie's face when he'd walked into the mall office. And the cuts and bruises on her face and body and the fear in her eyes and the way she'd collapsed in his arms.

"So, can we talk to him?"

"He's all yours. He's waived a lawyer and trial. He just wants to deal and walk."

Cole's mouth thinned. "I'd like to get my hands on him. He'd be lucky if he ever walked again."

Rick's hand closed over his partner's shoulder. "Easy, buddy. We don't need to make matters worse."

Cole nodded. But the anger continued to boil too close to the surface for comfort.

The door opened. Thomas Holliday looked up and then breathed a sigh of relief. He smirked and leaned back in his chair. The big guns had arrived. He could tell these guys were from Narcotics. No uniforms here. Plain clothes, cold eyes, and tight-lipped expressions gave them away.

Cole saw the smirk and resisted the urge to punch it off the punk's face. Cole shoved his hands in his pockets and stood back, breathing slow and deep to calm his rage as he and Rick made eye contact. Rick nodded.

"So, Holliday, it seems you want to tell us something special?" Rick said.

Rick Garza's soft tone and slight accent were deceptive. It was a valuable quality. He always played the "good cop" during interrogation. He had to. Cole Brownfield would never have fit the part. There was nothing soft or forgiving about the man. Not on the job. He'd seen too much on the street to be lenient with punks like this who'd sell their souls for a dollar.

Good-cop, bad-cop routine was a gimmick, but it was surprising how many times it worked.

Holliday nodded. All four legs of his chair hit the floor at once. He leaned forward, resting his arms on the table, and let his confidence show.

"What's in this for me," he asked.

"I might let you live."

The words were not what he'd expected. And they were not coming from the shorter, dark-eyed detective across from him. It was the tall man in the corner who'd spoken. A sudden chill chased across his spine. His eyes narrowed.

"What's the big deal?" he snarled.

"That's just it," Cole whispered, and stuffed his hands in his pockets. "No deals."

Thomas Holliday started to sweat. This wasn't going the way he'd expected. "But I can give you the names and places—"

"That's good, my man," Rick interrupted. It was time he took some control of the situation. He could feel Cole's anger behind him. It was a living, breathing thing and nearly out of control.

"You give us the information, and we'll inform the judge that you helped. But no deals."

"I don't get it! It was only a snatch. It didn't amount to much."

"It was also endangerment and assault and battery," Cole snarled. "The old woman at the beach had a heart problem. You snatched her medicine. If she'd died from the shock, we'd be talking manslaughter, and you assaulted a woman at the mall. There were witnesses.''

Thomas's hand slapped the top of the table with frustration. ''How was I to know the old lady had a bad ticker? And as for that bitch at the mall, she shouldn't—''

Cole yanked him out of the chair and had him against the wall before Rick could think to move.

''Don't call her a bitch...ever,'' Cole said softly. His hands tightened just enough around the suspect's neck to get his attention.

''Cole! Man, don't blow it.'' Rick's nervousness peaked.

''I'm fine,'' Cole said. ''I just want to make a point.''

Rick stood back. He trusted his partner. He knew he wouldn't do anything brutal. Thomas Holliday was the one capable of that. Not Cole Brownfield.

''What's the big deal?'' Holliday grunted.

''That woman at the mall...?''

Holliday nodded.

''She belongs to me.''

''Shit!'' The word was short and succinct. It said everything necessary to the situation. Thomas Holliday closed his eyes and cursed again. ''Just my luck.''

''Your luck consists of the fact that I'm an honorable man,'' Cole muttered. His breath fanned Holliday's cheeks.

Holliday looked up and saw his mortality flash before his eyes. It was a new thought, and one he didn't like to contemplate. He shrugged and breathed a quick sigh of relief as the officer turned him loose and helped him back to his chair.

"It's no big deal to me if I go up. It only means a place to sleep and three squares. Anyway, winter's coming."

Rick nodded and tried not to show that he'd almost lost faith in Cole's ability to maintain his presence of mind. If it had been his wife, he didn't know if he would have been that controlled.

"So, there's something you wanted to tell us?" Rick's smile was soft, but his eyes were not. He shared his partner's opinions of street scum.

Thomas Holliday shrugged. "Why the hell not? The judge might give me—"

"Don't count on it," Cole said.

Holliday started to talk.

It had been a long, but satisfying day. Cole turned into the driveway, killed the engine, and just for a moment, folded his arms across the steering wheel and rested his forehead against them. Peace enveloped him. He was home, and inside, a woman was waiting who made his world stay in orbit.

A car pulled into the driveway and parked alongside him. He looked up and smiled. His dad was getting his own world back in order. Golf clubs were riding shotgun beside Morgan Brownfield.

"Here, let me get those," Cole said as he shouldered the strap on the golf bag and accompanied his father into the house.

"What a day!" Morgan grinned. "I finally beat Henry Thomas. The old geezer won't admit it, but I beat him fair and square. He thinks I added my score wrong, but he wouldn't check it for himself." Morgan fairly chortled. "He didn't want it to be true, that's why!"

"Looks like we both had a good day," Cole said. "They arrested the man who attacked Debbie at the mall."

"Great!" Morgan cried. "This calls for a celebration. Debbie will be—"

Suddenly they looked at each other. Awareness spread. It was too quiet. Since the day she'd arrived, they'd never walked into the house without being met and greeted.

"Maybe she's asleep," Cole muttered, dropped the golf clubs, and sprinted for her bedroom.

Something told him she wouldn't be there. But he had to check. Her bed was empty. So was the pit in his stomach.

"She's not here," Cole said as he hurried back into the living room.

"Maybe Buddy knows where she is," Morgan offered.

"Bu-u-uddy!"

The echoing screech of his name sent Buddy running out of his room in panic. "What's on fire?" He could envision his precious computers going up in smoke.

"Where Debbie?" Cole asked.

The anxiety in his brother's voice told him this was no time to blank out. He vaguely remembered her telling him something... "Uh...um...I think..."

"Robert Allen, I haven't busted your lip since I was six and you were five, but so help me—"

"She went shopping." The reminder of pain was an incentive he could not ignore. "Now I remember. She asked me if I wanted anything from the mall. I told her—"

"She went to the mall...alone?"

Both men were in shock. They looked at each other and turned as one, intent on retrieving their Little Red before anything else happened to her...when she walked into the house. The blurred image of a cab driving away passed between her and the open door just before she slammed it shut.

"Hi, guys," she said as she staggered into the room with her arms full of sacks. "I hope you don't mind, but we're having chicken tonight, compliments of the Colonel."

She dropped two sacks into Morgan's arms and handed one to Buddy, unaware of the panic she'd caused.

"Wait till you see what I bought for the baby!" She handed another sack to Cole.

"Baby?" Cole was the first to speak, and he felt as

if he'd just walked into the twilight zone. She'd told him she was protected.

"Yes, baby." She was beginning to realize that something was wrong here. They were behaving as if they'd all had an overdose of bug spray from an orange grove. "You remember him, I'm sure. Your sister, Lily...remember? She had a baby. Your nephew...Morgan's grandson?"

"Oh! That baby," Cole dropped backwards into the nearest chair and held onto the sack she'd handed him as if it were a lifejacket that would keep him from sinking.

Debbie rolled her eyes and stepped back, taking a good look at the trio before her.

"What's going on," she asked.

"You went to the mall." Morgan's voice was slightly accusatory.

"You went to play golf," she retorted.

He blushed and dropped into a seat beside his son.

"Did you get my Pop Tarts?" Buddy asked, and then handed her his sack and bolted for his room when his father and brother glared at his question. He'd suddenly lost his appetite.

"What in the world is the matter with you?" Debbie asked. "Did you expect me to hide in this house for the rest of my stay, just because I got a busted lip? Besides, the man's been arrested. You called and told me that much, remember?"

The rest of her stay? Cole's stomach turned. That meant she'd be leaving.

Morgan decided that an exit at this point was wise and headed to the kitchen with the chicken and fixings.

Cole got up, dumped their sacks onto the floor, and wrapped her in his arms. "I'm sorry I overreacted," he said quietly. "But I came home and you were gone and—"

"You leave every morning," Debbie said. "You tell me you'll be back. I trust you to fulfill your word, Cole." She doubled up her fist and punched him gently in the chest. "You have to allow me the same."

"But you're so little, I guess that—"

"Bullets are smaller."

Her response shocked and silenced him. She was right.

"I suppose you're going to hold this over my head," he growled as he gave her one last hug before following her into the kitchen.

"Only if you hog all the drumsticks." She grinned, and then she knocked on Buddy's door as they walked by. "Buddy! You can come out now. And I did forget your Pop Tarts, but I brought you one of each of the desserts from KFC, instead."

He beat them both to the kitchen.

It was the witching hour. Cole had tossed and turned until his bed looked as if it had been turned inside out. All through their evening meal, Debbie had studiously ignored him. Oh, she'd laughed and talked and answered when spoken to, but she hadn't made eye contact once.

He wasn't sure what he'd done to warrant this treatment. But gut instinct told him that it was what he hadn't done that was causing her behavior. He'd caught the inference she'd made earlier about "her stay." He'd done nothing to insure that it was permanent. And it was time he did.

The hardwood floor was cool beneath his bare feet as he walked across the hall and paused outside her door. A thin string of light shown beneath, telling him that she was still awake. He knocked once, gently, and called her name. "Debbie, can I come in?"

"It's open," she answered.

He pushed the door inward, and what he saw pulled him into the room in a panic.

Her suitcases were open on the bed, some souvenirs she'd been accumulating were arrayed on table and bed, and some extra clothes were draped across a chair.

"Can't you sleep?" she asked without looking up. She didn't wait for his answer. "Me either. I got to thinking about what I'd accumulated since my arrival and wondered if I'd forgotten a gift for anyone. You know how it is…there's always a few friends back home who expect you to bring them a—"

"No!"

His denial was loud and sharp.

She stopped, turned around, and looked up. There was fear in his eyes.

"What?" she asked, and shrugged, sweeping her

arm toward the stuff on her bed. "Don't you ever take back little gifts for—?"

"You can't," he whispered, and pulled her into his arms.

"I can't what?" Debbie asked, struggling away from his grip. "I can't take back gifts, or I can't—"

"You can't go."

She stilled. Her pulse accelerated, and she closed her eyes, willing herself not to hope that he meant what she thought he meant. Then she looked up.

"Basically, the reason I came no longer exists. Your father is nearly well," she said softly. "No one's given me a reason not to leave."

Cole stared at the truth. It was hanging in the shadows of her eyes, accusing him and reminding him that he'd taken from this lady, but he'd given nothing back.

"I *will* stop you. I *am* giving you a reason."

His hands tightened at her shoulders as he leaned forward and swept his mouth across her lips. A faint memory of mint and roses clung to her skin, remnants of her nightly rituals. His mouth coaxed, and her lips opened beneath his touch. Slowly, in spite of herself, Debbie acquiesced. He drank from her sweetness and then couldn't suppress a groan as she tore herself away from his kiss.

"This is not a reason," she gasped. "This is pure, unadulterated need. There's no denying that sparks fly between us. But I choose not to live my life waiting for sparks. I know they can start fires, but you have to remember that fires always, finally, burn out."

"I love you."

The words came quietly, slipping from his lips as naturally and easily as breath is drawn in, and Cole wondered why he'd feared their coming.

She stopped. Motion ceased. For one long moment, time hung suspended, waiting for her reaction.

"Oh, Cole." Her voice shook. Debbie blinked, trying furiously not to cry. But it was hopeless. Her tears bubbled and fell.

"Don't cry," he begged as he scooped her up in his arms. "I didn't mean to make you cry." He feathered tiny kisses of repentance across her face.

"You win." Defeat was in her voice.

"I don't want to *win*, lady. I just don't want to lose."

He swept aside her neatly folded piles of packages and clothing, and fell into the middle of the bed with her beneath him. Her tears were on his face and her hands around his heart. The feel of her beneath him was more than he could stand. He wanted to come in. He'd been outside alone too long.

"Make love to me, Cole," Debbie whispered as her hands traced the strong outline of his shoulder blades.

"It would be my pleasure," he said. "And I promise, it will also be yours. Just don't ever leave me, lady."

"I promise," Debbie whispered. She looked up into dark eyes full of shadows and passion. "The lights are still on."

"When I'm with you, my lady, there is always light."

Poignantly, passionately, Cole began to touch her. And when she lay unclothed before him, bathed in the soft, muted glow of the lamp, he bowed his head at her beauty and wanted to shout with the joy of knowing she belonged to him.

"I love you so much," Debbie said, and lifted her arms.

"Thank God," he answered, and took what she offered.

Cole couldn't breathe and he was hot as a two-dollar pistol. He opened his eyes and knew the reason why. Sometime during the night, he'd discarded his covers and used Debbie instead. She was wedged lengthwise beneath him, sleeping the sleep of the innocent.

He smiled and yawned, then rolled over to face her and ran his hands through her hair, tousling her curls into even more disorder. The proximity of her backside was too tempting to resist as he cupped her in the palms of his hands and shook her from side to side.

"Hey, sleepyhead. It's late. I need to get up."

"Okay," she muttered. "Be careful. See you this evening." Then she snuggled her chin against his breastbone, intent on getting at least another hour's sleep.

He grinned. "Debbie, open your eyes."

She groaned, mumbling something about paying him back, and then gasped at her first sight of daylight.

"My gosh!" She elevated herself instantly, propping her arms on either side of his torso as she stared blankly around the room. "How did this happen?"

"You don't remember?" He leered and wiggled his eyebrows.

She blushed all over. "I remember plenty," she muttered, and started to move when his hands caught her hips and slipped her back onto a very interesting and sensitive spot that decided to make itself known.

"Oooh."

"My sentiments exactly," he groaned, and thrust upward.

Her eyes closed, her head tilted, and her hands grabbed hold of his shoulders to keep from falling forward. Awareness centered into one spiraling point of heat and pleasure that tightened and tightened until it burst, spilling Debbie forward. She collapsed into his arms.

For long, heart-pounding moments she was held within his strength. When her breathing resumed its normal pace and her sanity returned, Cole rolled her over beneath him, leaned up on one elbow, flicked a curl out of her eyes and whispered, "Good morning, my lady."

She blinked. *His lady!* What she wanted to be was his wife. Last night had been magic. She remembered everything…including the fact that Cole Brownfield had finally said he loved her. For now, it was enough.

"Good morning," she said. " I like the way you wake up."

He leaned his head back and laughed and laughed, his teeth a band of white against his dark, tanned skin. California sun had been good to this man.

"Thank you," he said. "I'm glad I could please."

"Oh, you pleased...very much."

Her husky whisper was giving him ideas that had to be saved for later. He was already going to be late for work. And he didn't give a damn. Rick could tease all he wanted. It had been worth it.

"I've got to go," he said, and gave her a quick but firm and branding kiss. "But I'll be back."

He rolled off the bed, retrieved his shorts, and had started out the door when he realized she'd remained too silent. It reminded him of what he'd walked in on last night before everything had happened. He turned and stared at the suitcase on the floor and the disarray of souvenirs in plain sight.

"I'll be here," she finally answered.

He nodded, satisfied that he'd gotten the answer he needed, and walked away.

It was much later in the day before he realized he'd never finished what he'd started to tell her last night. Yes, he'd told her he loved her. But he'd never asked her to marry him. He'd meant to. But her tears had driven everything out of his mind except regret that he'd made her cry.

He started to pick up the phone and then grinned to himself and dropped it back in its cradle. *What's the matter with you, Brownfield? You can't propose over a phone*. He shrugged and ran his hands through his hair in frustration. He needed to get a grip. There would be plenty of time later.

It was an assumption he shouldn't have made.

Chapter 10

Thomas Holliday was dead. The news had filtered through Narcotics like bad news always does—fast. And the fact that he was supposed to have committed suicide—in Narcotics, they weren't buying it.

Thomas Holliday was a thug and a thief and a coward. Cowards did not usually kill themselves. It was more common for someone to do it for them. That led Cole and Rick to suspect that someone on the outside had gotten wind of the fact that Holliday had talked.

"I wonder if Holliday had any visitors?"

Rick's question echoed a similar one that Cole just hadn't voiced.

"Maybe it's time we checked to see," Cole said.

They headed for the door.

Jackie Warren paced the floor. He didn't know whether to stay put or run. For the fifth time in as many minutes he went to the window and looked out, half expecting to see a police cruiser pulling up.

He'd heard the news this morning. He knew what the reporter had said. But he knew different. Holliday hadn't committed suicide, not technically. What he'd done was react to the message Jackie had been sent to give him. Holliday hadn't wanted to die. He'd just wanted to get away. Confined to a jail cell, he didn't have many options as to how to do that. Holliday had chosen the obvious.

"It's not my fault." Jackie Warren sniffed and shivered. He wasn't cold. He was scared. He was always scared.

The cops wouldn't understand. He knew it. But he'd had to do it. He'd had to deliver the message. His source hadn't given him any choice. And the cops didn't know how bad he'd needed that fix. At the time, he'd have sold his mother for it. As it was, he hadn't needed to. All he did was tell his source where Thomas Holliday was…and then deliver their message to him.

For the life of him, he couldn't understand why Holliday had become so all-fired important. First the cops had been looking for him and then—he shuddered.

"All I did was deliver a message," he told himself. "It's not my fault what happened. It's not my fault. It's not."

If he kept repeating that, maybe someday he'd come to believe it. And then again, maybe not.

The back door to his house opened. He heard the hinge squeaking on the screen. It couldn't be his sister, Nita. She was at work. It could only mean—

His eyes widened. His mouth dropped and he lifted a hand toward the man who walked into the room.

"I did what you asked," he said quickly. "I delivered the message just like you told—"

"I know," the man said. "And I've got something for you."

Jackie smiled with anticipation. He died with a smile on his face.

"This is the address," Rick said as Cole pulled up in front of the bungalow and parked.

The yard was in need of mowing. The shrubbery beneath the windows was overgrown and badly in need of trimming. Kids were playing in the yards across the street, and Cole frowned at their presence. If something went down, he didn't want any innocent people getting hurt.

"What do you think?" Cole asked. "Do we go to the front door together or...?"

"You take the high road, I'll take the low, my friend," Rick said, smiling at his own wit. "From what the boys in vice tell me, Jackie Warren is the type to run. I'll go around back, just in case, okay?"

Cole started to argue. Something about the whole thing was making him nervous. This had blown itself up into a lot more than an arrested purse snatcher committing suicide. Thomas Holliday's street connections obviously went deeper than just snatch and grab.

But Rick was already out of the car. Cole sighed, patted his jacket just to assure himself that his gun was in place, and crawled out of the car.

"Watch yourself," Cole warned. "I'm going to tell these kids to make themselves scarce. Wait for my signal before you come in the back."

Cole's quiet orders sent the children scurrying into the closest house. The once-noisy neighborhood was suddenly quiet.

Cole waved to Rick and then headed for the front door.

Rick nodded and started around behind the house to get in position.

Then a single gunshot rang out.

Everyone exploded into action. Rick grabbed the hand radio from his belt.

"Shots fired! Shots fired!" he yelled. He quickly gave their location and began to run.

As he ran, he ducked, and using the heavy, untrimmed shrubbery for cover, he made his way toward the front door. He dared one quick glance through the window. The thin curtain gave away only the faintest hint of a man moving through the front room.

Cole crouched, tested the doorknob and, when it turned freely, shoved the door open wide.

"Police!" he yelled. "Come out with your hands up."

A round of bullets sprayed through the open doorway, gouging huge chunks of concrete out of the porch. Cole's heart sank. It figured. The criminals always had the high-powered stuff, while the police were relegated to using regulation weapons that were often outmatched.

Footsteps pounded, running through the small house...running away from Cole's position. He quickly ducked inside the house, his gun held in position, his eyes searching the dim depths of the house for the assailant. He got one quick glimpse of a man lying on the floor. *Jackie Warren?*

The man was heading out the back. And then Cole remembered the bullets. He shouted at Rick as he ran.

Rick heard Cole yell. He positioned his gun and stance and waited for the door to open. Cole kept shouting something about bullets and cop killers, but he had no time to react to the warning.

The door was kicked open. The man exited on the run, his semiautomatic spraying the entire backyard as he made a dash for the high fence surrounding it.

Rick squeezed off one shot. It hit high on the man's leg. Just for a moment, he staggered, and Rick made his mistake. He stepped out of concealment.

Wild with pain and desperate to escape, the man turned. Rick felt the first bullet catch his side. There was no pain, only surprise. And then nothing at all.

Cole saw it happen. He came through the back door in time to see the man hit and Rick move.

"Look out!" he shouted. But it was too late. The man saw Rick and fired.

Cole shot. The gun bucked in his hands. Rick was down, and still the man kept shooting. Cole shot again, and the man turned. For one long moment, time suspended itself. Cole could see the green flecks in the man's eyes. He could see the pupils dilating with pain, and he saw the man's desperation. It wasn't over.

Bullets sprayed the ground in front of Cole. He emptied his gun, and finally...finally, the man went down. In the distance, Cole heard the sound of sirens. But they were going to be too late. The man was no more.

Then there was silence and the harsh gasps Rick was making as he struggled to breathe past the hole in his lungs and Cole's footsteps pounding across the yard.

Cole groaned softly. *Blood everywhere!* He grabbed for his radio.

"Officer down! I need an ambulance. Fast."

It was a policeman's worst fears. Hearing that call go out soon had a bevy of cruisers and several unmarked cars converging on the scene. But by that time, the ambulance had arrived and Rick was swiftly being carried away.

Cole was running beside the stretcher as they lifted his partner into the ambulance. He stood in shock, Rick's blood drying on his fingers, as they took Rick away.

"Tough one, Brownfield," one of the officers remarked as he walked up behind Cole. "Say, who got the one inside the house?"

Cole jumped. It was hard drawing himself back to the business at hand. He started to wipe his hand across his face and then took a look at its condition and shuddered.

"The guy out back," Cole muttered. "I don't suppose we'll ever really know why, but I suspect it was to shut him up."

The officer nodded, took a good, long look at Cole and stared at the blood on his clothing. "Maybe you need to get to the hospital and get yourself checked out," he offered.

Cole looked down in blank shock and shuddered. He felt sick to his stomach. "None of it's mine," he muttered, and walked away.

"We interrupt our programming to bring you this bulletin. Today, a detective from the Laguna Beach Narcotics Department was seriously wounded during a shoot-out in a local neighborhood. He was taken to South Coast Medical where the surgeons are now working to save his life. The identification of the officer has been withheld until—"

"No!"

Sheer terror overwhelmed her as Debbie stared at the television. She grabbed onto the nearest chair for support and stood in shock as she listened to the rest of the bulletin. Then regular programming resumed.

"Oh God, oh God." Her legs began to shake. *Morgan! He'll know what to—* "He's at the golf course," Debbie moaned softly to herself. Waiting was impossible. She knew where she had to be. She turned and ran.

"Buddy!"

The shock on his face matched the pain in her voice as the door banged against the wall. He leaped and grabbed her just before she dropped.

"Get me to South Coast Medical Hospital. I don't know where it is and I have to—"

"Are you sick?" Panic etched his face. This was not in his usual list of things to do and venturing away from his list was frightening, especially since Buddy was a man who needed to always be in control of his schedule.

Her chin quivered. Tears blurred her vision, but her grip on his arms was strong, and so was her voice.

"There was a bulletin on television. An officer from Narcotics was hurt during a shoot-out! They wouldn't give a name but it might have been—"

"I'll get the keys," Buddy announced. "You get in the car."

Debbie nodded, calming a bit with the knowledge that they were doing something besides waiting.

Buddy drove as if someone had just announced a sale at his favorite computer store. He turned corners at high speed and ran yellow warning lights, almost daring the Fates to slow him down. Debbie stared in amazement at the look of purposeful intent on his face. It was a complete turnaround from the vague expression he usually wore, and for the first time, she saw the resemblance between him and his brother, Cole.

His hand briefly touched her shoulder in a gesture of understanding, and then they roared through the next traffic light just before it turned red.

The hospital stood tall against the skyline, and her heart accelerated as they parked and began to run. When called upon, Robert Allen Brownfield had proved himself worthy.

They emerged from the elevator at a fast walk. A knot of people stood at the end of the hall. Someone was crying. Debbie began to shake all over again. Buddy slipped his hand beneath her elbow for support as they approached the group.

And then they walked into the waiting area and stopped. It was Tina Garza crying. Tears poured down her face as family and friends comforted her. Tina looked up and saw the pair who'd just entered the room. For just one moment, woman to woman, an understanding passed between them.

Buddy's hand on her shoulder refocused her attention. "It's Cole," he said quietly. "Over there."

Debbie took a deep shaky breath. "Thank God! Go tell Morgan he's all right. I'm staying with him. When we need to come home, we'll catch a cab."

Buddy nodded and started to walk away, his own relief making his legs a bit wobbly.

"Buddy." Debbie's voice was quiet, but he heard and turned. She hugged him tightly. "Thank you, darling," she said softly. "When it counts, you're the best."

He grinned and patted her awkwardly and, for one

silver second, thought of trading in his computers for someone like her. But reality reared, and he quickly dumped the thought and walked away. The only relationship he wanted was with a floppy disk and a good trade magazine. And when he felt the need, he could always eat a chocolate bar.

Debbie turned. Her attention focused completely on the tall man sitting alone against the wall, staring down at the floor. The dark stains on his clothing made her shudder. She knew what happened had been bad. Tears pricked at the back of her eyes, but she quickly ignored them. He didn't need tears. He needed to be held.

Cole stared blankly at the thread of green marble running through the off-white floor tiles and wondered whose job it was to put in the color. It was an inane thought, but it kept him from thinking about the fact that his friend and partner was in surgery, fighting for his life while his wife sobbed quietly in the opposite corner of the room, waiting to see if today she became a widow.

The ache inside him was blooming. He could feel it spreading in a cold, frosty path throughout his body. If he gave it its head, it would encompass him. He couldn't close his eyes. If he did, he kept seeing an instant replay of Rick going down, then of what had happened afterward. The two scenes flashed back and forth, caught forever in his memory in horrible perfection. He cursed quietly and buried his face in his hands.

"Cole."

It was soft. But it was the most welcome sound he'd ever heard. He stood, afraid to talk. Ashamed, because if he did, he might cry. He'd never cried in front of a woman except his mother in his life.

And then she was in his arms. He pulled her off her feet and up against him as a swift surge of grief overwhelmed him. "Rick...he's—"

"Sssh," she said. Her hands cupped his face as she rained tiny kisses against his eyes and cheeks. "I know, Cole. I know. And I'm so sorry."

He dropped them both into the chair, adjusted Debbie in his lap, and tried to ignore his overwhelming guilt at the fact that he was still alive.

She wrapped her arms around his neck and leaned against his shoulder as her hands moved across his face and neck, assuring herself that he was still in one piece and breathing.

"It happened so fast." The words came out of him in a swift bulky rage. "One minute Rick thought the situation was under control, and the next minute he was on the ground. The son of a bitch wouldn't stop shooting at Rick. I shot—" Cole shuddered and hushed, instantly.

Debbie's arms tightened around him. Suddenly she understood. Cole was not only dealing with the fact that his partner had been shot. He was trying to deal with the fact that he'd shot and, she suspected, killed the man who'd hurt Rick.

"It's your job, Cole. It's what you do."

He closed his eyes and buried his face in the curve of her neck. He knew that she was right. But he'd never killed a man before. And the man had given him no choice. Inside, the chill kept spreading.

"Mrs. Garza?" The doctor's voice had the same effect on the waiting area as water hosing down a dog fight. Silence reigned. Breathing stopped as all eyes turned to the man in surgery greens.

Tina stood, and then Cole was beside her.

"Your husband is a fighter. He's made it through surgery and is now in recovery. He'll be in ICU for a bit, but barring any complications, which at this early day I still can't rule out, his chances look good."

Tina sagged with relief and Cole's arms came around her. *"Madre de Dios,"* she moaned. "Thank you, God!"

"From the looks of you," the doctor said gently, "I think someone needs to take you home." He was referring to her obvious pregnant state. "Your husband won't know a thing for several hours. You can come back—"

"I'll stay," Tina said firmly. "I'm fine now. Now that I know."

He shrugged and nodded. "At least get off your feet," he ordered gently. "And eat something. You may not be hungry, but I suspect your *niña* will be." His hand was gentle on her shoulder as was his voice.

Cole spoke quietly but firmly. "She'll rest. And she'll eat. Her family will see to that."

The doctor nodded and then walked away. Tina turned and hugged Cole tightly.

"I know what happened, Cole. And I know you. You're blaming yourself for something that couldn't have been prevented. The captain has already been here. He told me everything, including the fact that you probably saved Rick's life, as well as some of the others. He said the man wouldn't stop coming or shooting." She bit her lips. "Sometimes, this job just stinks, *es verdad?*"

"*Es verdad,*" he agreed.

"Is someone looking after Enrique?" Debbie asked.

Tina nodded and welcomed Debbie's hug. "A neighbor took him to my mother's house. He will be fine." Then she smiled gently. "But thank you for asking. You're the first one who thought to ask about the rest of my family. I thank you for that. In times like this, sometimes they get misplaced."

Tina saw the strain on Cole's face. And she saw something else. He'd killed a man today. Despite the fact that the man was a criminal, despite the fact that the crook had shot first and nearly killed an officer, Cole was having a difficult time dealing with the fact that a man had ceased living because of him.

"Cole Brownfield," Tina said. He looked down into her knowing eyes and shuddered. "You did what you had to...and I thank you for my husband's life."

"If we'd been more careful, it might not have happened at all," he said quietly, and walked away.

"Go after him," Tina urged.

"I intend to," Debbie answered. "He's a strong man, but inside, he's very gentle. I suspect it's a hard combination to live with in a job like this."

Tina nodded and then turned back to her family. Her waiting had just begun.

Debbie followed Cole's retreat. "Do you have to go back to the station?" she asked.

Cole sighed and nodded. "I'll have to write a report."

"Can't it wait until tomorrow? It's late."

Cole looked down at his watch. It was nearly eight p.m. He looked outside. It would be dark soon. He shrugged as he looked down at his clothes. Dark stains reminded him of what had happened this day.

"I'll call in from the house," he said suddenly. "I need to take a bath first."

Debbie walked the kitchen floor. She stared out the patio door overlooking the backyard pool and looked up at the sky. It was cloudy and overcast. Rain would come before morning.

Morgan entered the kitchen. "You couldn't sleep, either? Are you waiting for him to come back from headquarters?"

She nodded and wrapped her arms around herself to keep from shaking. But her voice gave her away. "I've never been so scared and then so relieved in such a short span of time. In the space of an hour, my world nearly stopped." Her lips trembled as she walked into Morgan's open arms. "Thanks," she whispered, blinking back tears. "I needed that."

"It's the part of Cole that makes me the proudest and also the most afraid. Honor for what he believes in is as much a part of him as the color of his hair. He's a cop, Debbie. And a good one. Can you live with that?"

"I've already faced it," she said. "I've witnessed the long hours and coped, I think, reasonably well. I've seen him in action, and I've seen him hurting. But he won't let me share his pain."

Morgan nodded and patted her gently. "In time, he will...I think. Don't give up on him, honey. He loves you very much, you know."

Debbie never gave up on something she wanted. She walked away, unable to speak. The pain was too fresh for words.

The key turned quietly in the lock as Cole let himself inside. Raindrops ran off his hair and jacket onto the kitchen floor. He stepped out of his shoes and socks, draped his damp jacket across a stool, and walked barefoot through the house. It had been a long night. The paperwork was finally finished. A review of the shooting would take place, and then everything would go on as before. He had nothing to worry about.

But worry was all he could do. He kept seeing Rick's body buck from the impact of bullets. He shuddered, remembering the sound they made hitting flesh and remembering emptying his own gun into the man before it was over.

All that he'd feared from his job had happened in the space of one incident. His partner had been shot, and he'd killed a man. He took a deep breath and shuddered again.

I got rained on. It's only a chill.

But he knew better. It was getting to him, and he didn't know how to stop it from happening.

He opened the door to his room. The dim glow of a nightlight in his bathroom illuminated the room's interior, and he saw her. She was curled into a small wad, sleeping in the middle of this bed with her arms wrapped around his pillow. Every emotion he'd buried since the incident had happened came hurtling forward. They slammed inside him with rude, unforgivable force. There was no time to undress. He needed to get to her, and he needed it now. If he didn't make it to the bed and her arms, he'd come apart, from the inside out.

Droplets fell on Debbie's bare arms and face and yanked her awake. Cole was unwinding her from his pillow. She could feel his hands. They were shaking.

"You're home," she said sleepily. "I tried to wait up..."

"Just let me hold you," he pleaded softly. Agony was thick in his voice.

"You're wet," Debbie said. Her hands moved across his hair and across his cheeks as her breath caught at the back of her throat. It wasn't rain on his face.

"Come here," she said, and wrapped him in her arms.

In desperation, he clung to her strength and warmth. Words were not possible…or necessary.

Long after he'd finally relaxed in her arms and slept, Debbie was still awake, cradling his head against her breast. Her hands smoothed the nearly dry fabric of his shirt over and over in a gentle caress, a reminder that he wasn't alone. Often, his arms would tighten around her, and he'd begin to mumble. It was then that she'd know that he was starting to dream, to relive the horror of the incident all over again.

"Sssh," she whispered. "It's all right, Cole. I've got you, darling. And I'll never let you go."

His arms relaxed, his breathing evened, and Debbie sighed with relief. She threaded her fingers through his hair, combing gently against his scalp as he quieted.

Hesitant to acknowledge itself, morning finally dawned in a gray and rainy mood.

Exhaustion had finally claimed Debbie. Cole heard the steady rhythm of her heart before he opened his eyes and knew that he'd fallen asleep in her arms.

If I never have to move again, I'll be happy, Cole thought.

And then he looked down at himself and changed his mind. His clothes felt glued to his body. He couldn't remember the last time he'd slept fully dressed.

He shifted slowly, easing himself out of her arms. It only took a few seconds to undress, and then he was back beside her. She sighed softly in her sleep as he nestled her against him. Her arm slipped around his chest as her head fell into the hollow beneath his arm. Her hand was small and warm against his skin. He pulled the covers over them, slid his hand on top of hers, and closed his eyes.

They slept.

Morgan tiptoed down the hall toward Cole's and Debbie's rooms. The night had been long and traumatic for both of them, but in different ways, and he was anxious to check on them.

The door to Cole's room was ajar. He pushed it aside and had started to go in when he saw them. A mist of tears filmed his vision, and for one moment, he remembered his own wife and the precious mornings they'd spent in each other's arms.

They slept so peacefully. And Morgan suspected it had not come easy. He backed out and quietly eased the door shut. Last night was over, but he knew there would be many more nights during which Cole would suffer. What had happened yesterday wasn't something a man could quickly forget. It was something he would have to learn to live with. He prayed that Cole would let Debbie help him.

* * *

His hand cupped her breast and then moved slowly across her rib cage, feeling its way across her body like a man lost in a fog locating familiar landmarks to pinpoint his location before moving on to a chosen destination. She moaned and shifted her leg across him, recognizing the feeling that was beginning to build, knowing that it would only take a touch to send sanity flying.

He thrust slowly against her belly, sighing as the pressure intensified and moaning as he felt her mouth against his nipple. He rolled over and inside her before his eyes ever opened. It was with shock that he realized he hadn't been dreaming and that the woman beneath him, the woman he'd just entered, was real and not a figment of his imagination. She moved beneath him. Her body tensed, drawing him deeper, and he shuddered, realizing how quickly he was about to lose control.

Debbie's hands moved of their own accord across his backside. Her legs opened to accommodate him as she felt his muscles tensing beneath her fingers. She arched up in a silent plea for more and then gasped as he thrust. Dreams had never been this vivid. She opened her eyes and then smiled softly as she saw him staring down at her in shock. It wasn't a dream. And it was only beginning.

"I love you," she whispered as he began to move.

"Ah, God, lady...I..." Words became impossible.

Motion became fluid as their bodies merged perfectly into one instrument of pleasure. Nothing existed

for them at this moment but the need and the feeling
that they each knew was coming.

Heat intensified. Sunlight came through the over-
hanging clouds and burst through the curtain of his
room at the moment he spilled into her. Daylight had
never felt so good.

Weak from what she'd taken, strong from the
knowledge that it would happen again, he dropped his
head onto her breasts and nuzzled against their pil-
lowed softness. He finally was able to finish his sen-
tence.

"…I love you, too."

"Oh my God," Cole muttered. "Buddy cooked!"

"How can you tell?" Debbie asked as she walked
into the kitchen several hours later.

"I can smell it," he answered.

Debbie wrinkled her nose and tried not to laugh.
She finally got the message. She smelled a variety of
things, none of which seemed disgusting or burned,
but they all shared one thing in common. The kitchen
smelled like a candy factory. The air was permeated
with the scent of sugar…and chocolate.

"Wonder what it was?" she grinned, trying not to
laugh

"I can tell you," Morgan groaned as he walked into
the kitchen from the pool. "It was pancakes. Chocolate chip pancakes. And he ate his with chocolate
syrup." He shuddered. "I've been trying to swim
mine off ever since breakfast. My God, what did your

mother and I do wrong to produce an offspring like him?''

Debbie patted Morgan comfortingly as she went to prepare an antacid. "Here," she said, handing him the glass of bubbling effervescence. "And from my point of view, you did everything right. Yesterday, when it mattered, Buddy came through. And I don't want any of you to forget it. Do you hear me?''

Cole heard the strain in her voice and knew that yesterday had been a nightmare for them all. He watched her closely, searching her features for proof of his worst fears. He saw nothing but a small frown. And all he heard was a gentle warning that Buddy was not to be mistreated.

"I love my brother," Cole said gruffly. "But I don't have to love his cooking. Come on, we'll get something to eat on the way."

"Where are we going?" she asked as she headed out of the kitchen to get her purse and shoes.

"To the hospital."

His short answer sent her running to comply.

Chapter 11

Cole walked into the waiting area. His stomach lurched as Tina turned dull, lifeless eyes their way.

"What happened?" He could tell that last night had been rough.

"He took a turn for the worse around four this morning," she said. "They have him stabilized now, but for a while..."

Her lips trembled as she crawled up to a sitting position. She kicked the blanket the nurses had provided for her to the end of the couch and ran her fingers through her hair, smiling weakly as Debbie sat down beside her.

"I shouldn't have left," Cole said. A wave of guilt swept over him as he remembered where he'd spent the night...and how. Why should he have been enjoying life when Rick was fading?

"What would you have done?" Tina asked sharply. "Bullied the doctors? Cried harder than I did? Killed some one else?"

The color faded from her face. She clasped her fingers to her lips to call back the words, but it was too late. "Oh my God," she moaned, and jumped to her feet. She wrapped her arms around Cole's waist and buried her face against his chest. "I'm sorry. I'm sorry. You know my mouth—it has no brain, only a mechanism that makes it flap."

Debbie was sick. The look on Cole's face—if he'd been slapped, he couldn't have been more shocked. She wanted to shake Tina Garza, but knew that her words had come from exhaustion and fear. There was nothing she could do now but let Tina make her apologies and hope that when this was over, Cole had survived.

"It's okay, honey," Cole said, and patted her shoulder. He felt the slight protrusion of her belly pushing against him. It was only a reminder that Rick Garza had too much to live for to lose it now. "Last night was hell on everyone."

Tina turned away. Shame for what she'd done overwhelmed her. Cole was Rick's best friend, like a brother to her. And she'd done the unforgivable. She'd hurt the man who'd tried to save her husband's life.

"It's just this damn job," she cried. "It's inhuman."

Cole's expression froze. Debbie watched her world falling to bits before her eyes and knew that if she didn't do something now, it would be too late. Tina was simply mouthing Cole's sentiments. It's all she'd heard since she'd arrived from Oklahoma. Cops, marriages, and families don't mix.

She knew there were plenty of policemen and women who made marriages work…and work well. But the facts were there. There were also plenty that failed.

"Come with me," Debbie said. She slipped her hand beneath Tina's elbow. "Let's go wash up. When we come back, I'll fix your hair. When you put on some makeup, you'll feel like a new woman. Trust me."

Cole watched them walk away. He tried to block out what Tina had just said, but it was impossible. *Cops and marriages don't mix…don't mix…don't mix…*

They came back, but Cole was gone. Two members of Tina's family had just arrived to bring her fresh clothing and news of her son's night at the grandparents' home. For a moment, everything seemed almost normal.

"Did anyone see where Cole went?" Debbie asked.

A man, whom Tina quickly introduced as her uncle, spoke. "He's in Rick's room. The doctor was just here making rounds. He got permission." The last was said for Tina's benefit.

Tina slumped down into a chair and buried her face in her hands. "He doesn't need permission," she said softly. "He's as much a member of this family as any of us. I just hope he can forgive me for what I said."

"Don't," Debbie said softly. "Knowing Cole, he already has."

But Debbie was wrong. Cole hadn't forgotten a thing. And for the next five days, it festered inside of him until he was a fight waiting to happen.

"Dad, I'm going to be gone for a couple of days."

Morgan turned around in shock and dropped the shears he'd been using to trim the shrubbery in the backyard.

"Now? I thought you were taking a few days off since—"

"The man is dead. I couldn't stop it from happening, just like I can't make the world stop spinning, understand?"

"That isn't what I meant," Morgan answered just as sharply.

Cole stuffed his hands in his pockets. The grim expression on his face darkened. "I know it," he said. "And I still jumped all over you anyway. That's why I need to get away. I've got to get back to work, get back on the street..."

He stared into the clear, nearly blue-white waters of the pool. "If I don't do it now, I may never be able to face it again."

Morgan hugged his son. "I didn't realize it was bothering you this much," he said. "I'm sorry."

Cole shrugged. "Nothing anyone can do...except me."

"Does Debbie know?"

Cole turned away. He didn't answer.

"Cole...dammit! Does she?"

"No!"

It was harsh, but it was clear. Cole started into the house.

"Are you going to tell her, or are you leaving that up to me, too?" Morgan was angry. He couldn't face being the one to deliver her hurt.

"I can't," Cole shouted. "God dammit, I can't." The pain was thick in his voice. Tears welled, but refused to flow.

Morgan was sick. He relented instantly, but it was too late. His son was already walking out the door.

Debbie stood in the shadows of the hallway as tears ran blindly down her face. She almost called Cole's name aloud, but she was afraid if she opened her mouth, nothing would come out but a scream. She'd heard everything.

Buddy leaned against the door to his room and stared at the computers winking at him from across the room. He needed to fix this. But he didn't know how to fix broken people, only machines. This was out of his realm of expertise. And then he heard Debbie sobbing. A small streak of Brownfield spirit made him grip the doorknob and open the door with a hard, vicious yank.

Debbie stared, surprised by the unlikely vehemence

with which Buddy was moving. He grabbed her by the arm, and began pulling her toward the front door.

"What are you doing?" she said.

He stopped, a stunned expression spreading on his face. He looked down at the firm grip he had on her arm and quickly released it with an awkward apology. "Ummm...I just thought...if you weren't too..." He took a deep breath, yanked his shirttail from his pants and swiped it across her face, drying tears and streaking makeup in one fell swoop. "We're going to get some ice cream," he said.

Debbie's heart skipped a beat. *Oh Buddy! You dear! Why didn't I fall for someone like you? Someone with no complications?* And then her heart answered her own question. *Because I didn't fall in love with my head, I fell in love with my heart. And my heart belongs to Cole.* She shuddered. *I just don't think he wants it anymore.*

"Thank you, Buddy," she said. "I think I'd like that. Maybe your dad would like to come?"

He smiled, happy that his suggestion was being met with so much appreciation. "I'll get him," he said, and lurched toward the backyard.

Debbie sighed as she watched him hurry away. At least the rest of the family still loved her. It was small comfort, but it was a comfort nonetheless.

The doorbell was ringing and ringing. Debbie dropped her mixing spoon back into the bowl, ignoring the fluff of flour that poofed over the edge and onto the counter as she ran to answer the persistent summons.

She peered through the peephole and then screamed with delight. The door flew back with a thud and for just a moment the sunlight was blocked by a very tall man wearing a weary smile and juggling a multitude of bags. The woman standing beside him had a bag over one shoulder and a baby on the other.

"Lily! Case! Why didn't you call? Why didn't you tell us you were coming? Someone could have met you at the—"

Case dumped the bags and scooped her up into his arms, laughing as he moved her over to make room for the rest of his family to come in.

"You haven't changed a bit, Deb. You still talk faster than you walk, and that's saying something," he said. "Besides you know Lily. The moment the doctor said she could travel, we were on the plane. She's been very worried about Morgan."

"Lily! You look great!" Debbie said. "Your dad's next door. He's going to be so excited." And then her expression changed as worry tinged her voice. "I'm in your old room. It'll take me a little while to get my stuff out of—"

"Leave it," Lily said calmly. "I spent my entire life across the hall from my big brother. I know how cranky he can be in the morning. I don't think he'd appreciate listening to his nephew crying during the night. Are the twins still gone?"

Debbie nodded.

"Good. We'll take their room. It's bigger anyway."

It didn't take long for bag, baggage, and family to be moved into the Brownfield residence. Case wandered back through the house, taking note of the layout and the inviting blue waters of the backyard pool, and found Debbie staring blankly into a bowl of partially mixed dough.

"Did you forget what you were doing?" he teased as he slid a gentle hand across the back of her neck. "You've been a godsend to us, honey. I can't tell you how much we appreciated you coming out when you did. But as you can see, as soon as the doctor gave her the go ahead, Lily was packed. All I could do was follow."

Debbie looked up into those dearly familiar big-sky eyes, so blue they made her heart ache, and promptly burst into tears.

"Well, hell," Case said softly and wrapped her in his arms. He didn't know what had caused this outburst, but during the last few months, he'd learned that it didn't matter what caused them, the proper procedure for healing them was a hug.

"I finally got the baby down," Lily said as she walked into the kitchen and then stopped short. She caught her husband's frown and shrug, and sighed. If Deborah Randall was in tears, she suspected her brother's absence had something to do with it.

Before Lily could offer advice or condolences of any kind, her father's voice sent her spinning.

"Lily Kate! You're home," he said, and engulfed her in a warm, welcoming hug.

Debbie jerked away from Case, mortified that she'd lost control, and quickly swiped at her tear-stained face, unwilling for Morgan to see her in this condition.

"And Case! It's great to see you, son. I hate to be rude, but where's my grandson?"

Debbie stood back as the proud parents quickly ushered Morgan to the bedroom. He beamed as he looked long and hard at the tiny baby sleeping soundly on the bed.

"He looks like you, doesn't he, Case?" Morgan was overwhelmed by the emotion of seeing such a tiny bit of his own immortality.

"Yes, Dad, he does," Lily answered. "And I can't wait for him to wake up so you can see his eyes. They're so blue..."

"All new babies have blue eyes," Morgan teased.

"Not like these," Lily said. "He has his daddy's eyes."

Case still couldn't get over the joy he felt at hearing those words, *his daddy's eyes*. He couldn't believe that he and Lily were parents. But the proof was there in the middle of the bed.

Debbie started forward when the phone rang in the other room.

"I'll get it before it wakes the baby," she said, and dashed down the hallway to the phone on the table. "Hello!"

Her voice was soft and breathless. Cole groaned and

cursed the Fates as he realized he was finally going to have to talk to her, even if it wasn't face to face.

"It's me," he said.

Debbie almost dropped the receiver. It was the first time in thirty-six hours that she'd heard his voice, and even now, he didn't sound a bit better than he had when he'd stormed out of the house.

"So it is," she said shortly, and then waited.

Cole cursed softly. This wasn't going to be easy. "I just thought I'd call and let you know Rick is out of the woods."

"That's wonderful," she said. "Are you still working...or are you just running?"

The sarcasm was not lost on him. It made him defensive...and that was not a wise move. "You don't understand a thing about it," Cole said.

"That's possible." Tension hummed between them. "I can't read your mind. And you certainly haven't talked to me about anything. You slept with me, but you damn sure haven't talked."

"Listen, lady—" he began.

She cut him off short. "No, you listen," she cried. "I know you're going through a bad time, Cole. So is Rick. So is Tina. But they haven't shut each other out. They've been leaning on each other for strength."

"How would you have felt if it had been me instead of Rick? How would you like it if we'd had children and you were left alone to raise them?" Cole argued.

Debbie heard the pain in his voice. But he wasn't listening to her. She had to make him understand. "I know one thing, Cole Brownfield. I would be proud to call you husband. And I'd be strong enough to raise our children alone…if I had to. But we won't have to worry about any of that now, will we? You're too busy trying to fix what never happened. You're too busy assuming that I'd be a quitter." Her breath caught in a sob as she finished. "Well, I'll tell you something, mister. I'm not the quitter. You are."

Case stood quietly at the end of the hall, listening. He wanted to wring his brother-in-law's stupid neck.

He'd never known a family as determined to do everything their own way as the Brownfields. It had taken years off his life, just worrying if Lily would ever get over her hang-up about being scarred long enough to see that he loved her just the way she was. The scars were gone now, but Case hadn't forgotten the pain of wondering. He could tell his friend Debbie was suffering the same way. He headed toward her.

Debbie looked up, saw Case coming down the hall with a determined expression on his face, and thrust the phone into his hands. "Here, you talk to him. I don't have anything else to say." Then she walked away with her head held high and ignored the fact that she was dying inside.

"I don't know what the hell is going on," Case growled into the phone. "And I don't want to. But if you don't do something about it, Cole, I'm going to have to punch your face."

It hadn't taken Case Longren long to get to the point. Cole smiled to himself as he hung up the phone.

It was what he'd most admired about the tall Oklahoma cowboy the first time they'd met.

In his heart, he knew that Debbie was right. *He* was the one running from the truth. And the truth was, he loved her to desperation. If he lost her, it would kill him.

Then what the hell am I doing? If I don't get myself together and get home, I've already lost her.

Cole walked back toward his desk. He stared at the mountain of paperwork and wanted to strike a match to it. With Rick gone, he was doing twice the work with half the results. *Damn, but I miss you, buddy. And thank God that you're getting well.*

He made a mental note to swing by the hospital later and check up on the Garzas before going home. *It should be interesting to go home tonight and have everyone watch me make a fool of myself,* he thought, then shrugged. *What did it matter? I've already acted like a fool. One more time isn't going to make that much difference.*

Buddy sat in silent awe, staring at the tiny bit of humanity wiggling around on his brother's bed. The baby's hair was thick and dark and stood up like new-mown grass. His fingers itched to touch, but he feared to make the move. There was no blinking cursor on this tiny little man to tell him where to begin.

The baby began to squeak. That gave him the impetus to introduce himself.

"Hello, Charlie Longren," he said quietly. The baby ceased wiggling instantly as his little blue eyes searched blindly for the location of the unfamiliar voice. "I'm your uncle. My name is Robert Allen Brownfield, but you may call me Uncle Buddy...when you learn to talk."

The baby squiggled and kicked. The soft white blanket covering his legs slipped down and with one more kick, it was in a wad at his feet.

"Yes," Buddy said, conversationally, "I can see that you're very strong. That's good. Obviously like your father, of course. I never was much for feats of physical prowess."

The baby shoved a fist toward his mouth and grimaced when the fist went sailing spastically by.

"You'll get the hang of it eventually," Buddy said, as if he were talking to one of his peers. "Personally, when I was younger, I preferred a thumb. However, you may choose a finger or a combination of several. I understand some do."

Lily blinked back tears. She'd walked into the room, certain that the baby was probably awake and then caught her breath at the sight. Buddy was in love. It was probably going to be his first and only, but that made it all the more special.

"Lily!" Buddy said. "I didn't know you were here."

"I just arrived," she said quickly, not wanting him to know that she'd overheard any of the man-to-man talk that had been going on.

He nodded, satisfied that his secrets were safe. "I think he likes me," he said softly.

The baby began to fuss after hearing Lily's voice.

"He's probably hungry," Lily said. "I brought his bottle. Do you want to feed him?"

Buddy's eyes dilated. His mouth dropped, and his fingers twitched as he considered the possibility. Finally, he answered. "Yes, I believe I would. But you'll have to show me how to pick him up. I wouldn't want to damage him."

Lily grinned. "You won't damage anything, Robert Allen. Just scoop and balance everything wiggling. I'll hand you the bottle."

Buddy stood and walked around the bed, carefully measuring the best angle to make his descent and, when he was satisfied that he'd figured it out, leaned over and deftly lifted the baby from the bed.

It was a perfect lift-off. Lily had expected awkwardness, even nerves. She should have known better. When Buddy did something, he always did it to perfection. The baby was in good hands.

"Sit down," she said, "and cuddle him. Here's his bottle."

"Thank you, Lily. Do I insert it now or...?"

The baby began to fuss at being held in the nursing position.

"Yes, Buddy. Insert it now." She tried not to grin at his terminology.

The bottle went in, and Buddy's face lit up. "Well, now, Charlie. I'll bet that just hits the spot. When

you're a little older, I'll treat you to some of my favorite drinks. There's one with two scoops of chocolate and—''

"We call the baby Morgan," Lily corrected. But
her brother wasn't listening. As far as Buddy was concerned, the baby was Charlie. She suspected as time
passed, he would be Charlie to everyone. Buddy had
a way about him.

Cole walked down the hospital corridor, wincing as
a nurse hurried past with a capped syringe in her hand
and a look of determination on her face. He was heart-
ily glad he wouldn't be on the receiving end of that
needle. Soft laughter drifted out into the hall. It was
coming from Rick's room.

Cole opened the doorway and paused unobserved.
It gave him an opportunity to see for himself how well
his partner was healing.

The burden of guilt that he'd been living with, the
constant reminder that he'd killed another man,
seemed to lessen. In fact, the longer he watched Rick
and Tina together, the easier it became to face the fact.
Somehow it was finally justified in his mind. If that's
what it had taken to keep a good man like Rick Garza
alive, then it had been worth it. He stuffed his hands
in his pockets and allowed himself a long, slow sigh.

It was then Rick saw him standing in the doorway.
"Hey, buddy. Don't be a stranger. Come in and see
what Tina has."

Cole grinned. "I heard the laughter all the way down the hall. What's so funny?"

Tina looked up and smiled. "We're laughing at a picture Enrique drew. It is of the little girl next door. We're trying to decide whether to move now or wait until Enrique is a little older before we panic."

Cole looked puzzled. Tina explained.

"We think he's in love. He drew a picture of the girl and put bats all over her clothing. It's a sure sign he likes her, you know. Only the best rate bats."

Cole laughed. He remembered the boy's infatuation with his hero, Batman.

"Better move now, love is hell," he warned.

Tina stopped laughing and stared point blank. "What's going on?" she asked sharply. And then she looked past Cole into the open doorway. "And where's Debbie? I haven't seen her in days. Have you?"

Cole frowned and stuffed his hands in his pockets.

"Tina..." Rick's warning was soft but firm. He grasped her hand. "You're got enough to worry about without interfering with Cole's business."

"It's my business, too," she said. "You don't understand. When you were so sick...I...I lost my temper and said some hurtful things. And I think—" she looked up at Cole with tear-filled eyes "—I think it just may have given Cole the wrong idea."

"Tina! You didn't lose your temper? I'm shocked! What will Cole think?" Rick grimaced as he shifted to a more comfortable position. And then he continued with a sarcastic grin. "Of course you lost your temper. You always do. It's one of the things I love most about you."

Cole listened. Fascinated by their ability to laugh, as if the last few days had never happened.

"But you were so frantic," Cole said to Tina. "You were blaming the job and—"

"And you. Tell the truth," Tina whispered, ashamed of herself but unwilling to ignore what she'd done. And then she shrugged. "I can't help it. It's just my nature. When bad things happen, I always have to blame something...or someone. Then I can get on to the business of fixing it."

"What if this couldn't be fixed?" Cole asked, unwilling to look at his partner's face. But he had to know.

Tina slid her hand beneath her husband's. Her eyes teared as he gave it a gentle pat.

"Then I would have had ten good years to remember and two children to love," she answered. "I knew when I married Rick that he was going to be a cop. I accepted it then. What has happened has changed nothing, except maybe it makes me appreciate him more."

"If you have love, Cole, nothing else matters," Rick said quietly.

Cole stared at the truth on his partner's face. His stomach tilted. He had the strongest urge to go home. Suddenly, seeing Debbie would come none too soon.

"Really glad to see you doing so well, Rick. Everyone sends their best. I've got to be going now. I'll see you later.''

He made a hasty exit from the room and missed the knowing looks that passed between the Garzas. Tina leaned her head down on her husband's arm and kissed his hand. She had much to be thankful for.

It hit him like a ton of bricks. The chaos was complete. Cole was speechless at the sight that met him when he walked into the house.

The baby was crying.

Morgan came running from the kitchen with a heated bottle full of baby formula.

Case was competently patting his son's behind, trying to soothe him until the arrival of food.

Buddy had disappeared into his room, convinced that dirty diapers and burping babies left a lot to be desired. He'd decided to admire and cuddle when the opportunity arose, and wait until Charlie could communicate on a higher level than shrieks.

Cole grinned. *Now this is what I call, "coming home."*

"Hi, everyone,' he said. "So, this is my nephew. Hi there, fellow," he crooned, and stroked the baby's crumpled cheek. His little mouth turned automatically toward the touch, and for a moment, his crying hushed. "Aren't things going your way today? Boy, can I ever sympathize. Where's Lily?" he asked, wondering where the new mother was in all this melee.

"Taking a shower," Case said, and resisted the urge

to sock his brother-in-law. "If I were you, I'd be a whole lot more concerned about where Debbie was."

Cole's smile disappeared. The sick feeling came back into his stomach with rude force. "What the hell do you mean?" he asked.

Buddy sauntered into the room. "She's gone."

Morgan thought fast and shoved a chair behind his son's knees just before he hit the floor.

"What do you mean...gone?"

Case already regretted the hasty way he'd announced the fact. They'd all suffered a similar panic only moments before, but his son's distress had taken first place in the sequence of things to be done.

"He means she's packed. She's gone. She's on her way back to Oklahoma. That's what he means," Case said shortly. "I told you things were bad. It took you damn long enough to show up and fix them. Looks like you were an hour late and a dollar short."

"Oh God!" Cole groaned. "When did she leave? Does anyone know when her flight leaves? Maybe I can catch her before—"

"She won't be on the plane."

All eyes turned toward Buddy's bland announcement.

"What do you mean?" Morgan asked. He'd spent too many years seeing that same expression on his son's face at the worst possible moments.

"I mean, she'll miss her flight, that's what I mean," Buddy said, mouthing each word slowly and distinctly, as if his family's elevators didn't go all the way to the top. *It is a trial, living with people who can't understand the simplest facts,* he thought. "Are there any brownies left?" he asked of no one in particular, and started out of the room.

Cole grabbed him by the arm and plastered him against the wall. The hard stare was unmistakable. Buddy began to get nervous. His brother was mad.

"How do you know she'll miss her plane, Buddy?" Cole's voice was very quiet. "What have you done?"

That he'd done something, there was no doubt. Cole had also known his brother too long to miss the look of feigned innocence.

"Well, it was obvious that you weren't going to do something," he accused, and pushed Cole's hands off his arms. "So it was left up to me, that's all."

"I repeat," Cole said. "What the holy hell did you do?"

"I put my castle and princess computer game in her luggage, that's all," Buddy said.

Cole's mouth dropped. He slapped his forehead with his hand to keep from slapping his brother instead. "You don't mean the—"

Case was lost. He didn't understand these Brownfield men. He was still having a hard time understanding the woman. "I don't get it," he asked Morgan and Cole. "What's the big deal about a game? Everyone has them."

"Not like Buddy's," Cole said. "It's one of a kind, and it looks like a remote control for detonating a bomb. Remember when we came to Oklahoma last year? Well, we spent several hours in LAX trying to explain that our brother is a harmless nut.''

Cole spun around and slammed his fist against the wall. "For the love of God, Buddy. You'll get her arrested, and you know it. What were you thinking?"

Buddy looked at them as if they'd suddenly lost their minds. He couldn't understand it. How could he have a family so dense? "I was thinking that you love her but that you're terribly stupid."

"Oh," Cole said. There was nothing else to say. He patted the baby's tiny back. "It was nice meeting you, Charlie," he said quickly. "I'll be back later. I've got a plane to catch."

"She won't be on the plane," Buddy reminded him.

"She will kill us all," Cole said, and made a run for the door.

Chapter 12

If anyone had told her she'd be running away, Debbie would have called him a liar. But the truth was, she'd met her match. It was time to face facts, no matter how much they hurt. Cole might love her, but he didn't trust her. And without trust, there was no love.

Tears sprang into her eyes. Her heart ached. Shaky legs carried her through the thick throng of people coming and going in the busy Los Angeles airport terminal. More than once she was jostled by an impatient traveler hurrying to catch a plane. But she didn't care. The farther she got from Cole, the worse she felt.

Leaving had been her last option. There was a limit as to how long a woman could humiliate herself for love. Everyone in the family knew she loved Cole.

And everyone also knew that Cole was doing nothing about it. It was going to kill her, but come hell or high water, she was getting on that plane.

The bag slipped on her shoulder and she gave it another hitch, relocating it to a strong position. All of her other luggage had been checked, but she'd been unable to trust her breakable souvenirs to the baggage handlers.

The closer she got to the checkpoint, the heavier it became. Debbie knew that she was being weighed down by more than souvenirs and hair spray. Guilt was weighing heavily on her heart as well as her mind.

I shouldn't have left him, she thought. *But what else could I do?*

"Place your purse and bag on here, miss," the attendant ordered as Debbie stepped up in the line.

She complied and walked through the metal detector to meet her bags on the other side of the security X ray. She was standing, staring down at the floor, lost in thought, when alarms began to go off and the attendant shouted and grabbed her arm.

"Get some more security here, on the double. We've got a problem," he ordered.

Debbie gaped. Two uniformed officers appeared and grabbed her, one on either side. With her bags in tow, the trio began a quick walk toward an area designated as off limits to ordinary travelers. People pointed and stared.

"What?" she gasped. "I don't understand. You've made a—"

"Just save it, miss," one of the officers ordered. "You can explain it to the chief."

Debbie rolled her eyes, caught a glimpse of a clock on the wall as she was all but dragged through the hallway, and knew without a doubt that she would not make her plane. She didn't know about high water, but hell had come calling.

Cole made the entire run to the airport with lights flashing, moving unsuspecting citizens out of the way in a desperate attempt to save Debbie the embarrassment of being arrested. The traffic on the freeways was, as usual, a tow-trucker's delight.

The exit leading to the airport finally came into view. He glanced down at his watch and knew that whatever was going to happen already had. Either Buddy's sabotage had failed and Debbie was gone, or she was under arrest. Neither was an option he wanted to consider.

He chose airport parking. If Debbie was under arrest, it would take hours to straighten out this mess. He could still remember his own family's nightmare trip, when they'd had to try to convince the authorities that Buddy's invention was nothing more deadly than a hand-held computer game. And, if by chance Debbie was already gone, he was going to be right behind her. Either way, he wouldn't be needing his car for some time to come.

Stuffing the claim ticket in his pocket, he began to jog. By the time he reached the terminal, he was in an all-out run. Several people stared at the tall, suntanned man dressed in blue jeans and sneakers. And quite a few noticed how well his Forty-niners T-shirt molded to his physique. But it was all they saw. He was merely a blur through the crowd.

Cole was running. One quick look told him her flight had been delayed. *Oh Lord! That means she's been arrested, and they're probably searching baggage.*

What he had to do now was get to security, and he knew right where it was. He should. He'd spent the better part of three hours there himself.

"You can't go in there," a guard shouted as Cole sprinted down a hallway.

He stopped, breathing hard, and dug in his pocket and flashed his badge. "Detective Brownfield, Laguna Beach Narcotics," he said quickly. "Can you tell me, in the last hour or so, has a young woman been arrested?"

The guard grabbed Cole by the arm and asked, "What do you know about it? And let me see that badge again."

I can see I was right. "Just take me to security," Cole asked. "I can explain everything."

"I seriously doubt it," the guard said.

"Believe me," Cole sighed, as they started down a long hallway, "I can."

Debbie stared at a point just past the officer's shoulder and stifled the urge to scream. She'd been answering the same questions for nearly an hour. It was obvious that they either needed hearing aids or didn't believe her. She opted for the latter.

"So, Miss Randall," Officer Tillet droned, "if you claim you know nothing about how this got in your luggage, maybe you *can* tell me what it does." He pointed to Buddy's computer game, careful not to touch any of the buttons and accidentally activate anything deadly.

She leaned forward, resting her elbows on the table, and drawled, "All I know is that, if you don't turn it on, you can't rescue the princess."

Tillet frowned. *Must be some kind of code. One never knows about radical factions and their crazy plans to save the world.* His pulse soared. This would mean a promotion for sure if he'd accidentally stumbled onto a plot by the IRA to harm the Royal Family.

"Princess, huh? As in Princess Di, maybe? Where were you headed anyway, London?"

"Right," Debbie said shortly, "by way of Oklahoma City, Oklahoma?"

He looked taken aback. "Check that out," Tillet ordered. One of the men scurried from the room.

"If you claim not to know anything about how it got in your luggage, then how do you explain your knowledge of it?" He had her there. He just knew it.

"I didn't say I'd never seen it. I just said, I didn't know Buddy had put it in my bag."

Now we're getting somewhere. She's about to name an accomplice. They always do when they're about to be caught. They never want to go down alone. "So, exactly what's your buddy's real name?" He leaned forward and pinned her with a stare.

"Robert Allen Brownfield," Cole said. "And unfortunately, he's my brother."

Cole was silent, waiting for a response to his announcement. He'd probably get arrested, too. *The Chief would love that,* Cole thought, picturing his boss's face when he tried to explain this mess back at the P.D.

Debbie leaned back in her chair, covered her eyes with her fingers, and pressed tightly. *Thank God!*

Cole saw her actions and felt the floor tilt beneath him. *She's furious. She's never going to forgive me or anyone claiming a remote relationship to a Brownfield.*

Tillet jumped. "Who's he?" he asked.

Cole reached for his pocket. Two officers reached for their guns. He rolled his eyes. "In my pocket, please," he said.

An officer handed the wallet to Tillet.

A detective...with the Laguna Beach P.D.? What's going on here? They'd better not mess with me. This is my territory. I won't have anyone claiming credit for something I've—

"Brother?" What the detective had said finally registered. "What's going on here?" Tillet asked.

Cole shrugged free of his restraints and claimed his badge. "If I may..." he leaned forward and picked up the offending black box.

Everyone jumped back and several more officers drew their weapons. "Don't shoot," he drawled, "or I'll never get that damned princess out of the tower."

The machine came to life beneath his fingers, and for the first time, he was thankful that this was one of Buddy's games he knew how to work.

Lights came on, a computerized version of trumpets blared, and a tiny, robotic figure appeared on the small screen. It thrust and parried as the game's instructions were given to proceed.

"Prince Robert," Cole grinned, as he introduced the dashing little figure. He looked at Tillet and asked, "Do you want to take the road to Challon or go by water? I'll warn you, if you go by water, there's a hell of a monster just past the first set of cliffs that'll eat your damned boat every time."

The men assembled started to grin. One even stepped forward and held out his hand. "I'll give it a try," he offered. "I'm real good at—"

"Get back to your post," Tillet ordered. He hated days like this. "Miss Randall, I'm sorry you've been detained unnecessarily, but I'm certain you understand our position. We'll give you a personal escort to the plane and see that you get on it. It'll take about a half an hour to reload the baggage, and then you may resume your trip in peace." It was obvious that he'd be happy if he never saw her again.

Cole stepped forward. "That won't be necessary," he said. "If you'd be so kind as to get her bags off the—"

Debbie spoke. "Don't remove a thing. And I'll get myself to the proper gate." She walked out the door.

No!

Cole bolted after her.

Tillet sank down onto the nearest chair and stared at the figure of Prince Robert going down for the third time. A grinning dragon appeared on the screen and then a series of trumpets blared. The dragon had won. The princess was still in the tower, and Tillet was going to be the laughingstock of the week.

"What do you think you're doing?" Cole yelled, ignoring the curious stares sent their way.

Debbie didn't answer. She just kept walking.

"So, you're quitting! It doesn't surprise me," he shouted. "I always knew that my being a cop bothered you."

Debbie frowned. *that's part of his trouble,* she thought. *He doesn't know what I think. He just imagines he does.* She never slowed down.

"If you think I'm going to get down on my hands and knees. If you think I'm going to swear to quit being a cop just for you…"

She didn't respond and Cole picked up his pace. Just as they reached her loading gate, he grabbed her by the arm and hauled her around. "If you think I'm going to let you get on that plane, you're crazy."

He wasn't just warning her. He was desperate and determined. She knew when she'd met her match. But there was no use in spoiling this by admitting it too soon. She shifted gears.

"I suppose you *could* stop me...this time. But there'd always be a next, and a next and a—"

"Why?" The heartbreak in his voice was evident. "I love you, lady. I'm sorry my family caused you so much trouble. I'm sorry I've hurt you." Fear overwhelmed him as he stared at the lack of expression in her eyes. "It doesn't matter to you, does it? If I don't change my occupation, this conversation is null and void."

"I don't remember asking you to quit being a cop." The sharp tone of her voice got his attention...and everyone else's within a ten-yard radius.

Cole rolled his eyes. She was going to make him beg. He was nearly at that point anyway. "Just because you didn't ask doesn't mean I can't read between the lines," he snarled.

"I don't think you can read directions to the nearest bathroom, Cole Brownfield. Don't you dare stand there and tell me you read what I'm feeling."

She huffed herself up with a vengeance. Cole would have sworn he just saw her grow. It was impossible. But she *was* really mad.

"Then what's the big deal? If you love me, and if I love you, then why won't you marry me?"

"Probably because you never asked," Debbie said.

Several people laughed quietly, and one woman sniffed into the stunned silence of the crowd, obviously moved by what she would later claim was better than any soap opera any day.

Cole forgot to breathe. She was right! He'd never said the words. But dear God, he'd thought them, right up until Tina Garza had lambasted police work as being responsible for Rick's condition. He knew that she'd later recanted, but he hadn't been able to get past her fury. All he'd done was transpose her behavior onto Debbie without giving Debbie the benefit of the doubt.

Cole slid his arms around her, clasping her tightly against him, and nestled her against him. He rested his chin on the top of her head. "I meant to," he said quietly.

Debbie shrugged. "But you didn't." She spoke around a shirt button. Her nose was smashed against his collar bone, but she didn't care. She'd never thought Cole would hold her again. This was heaven. But he didn't deserve to be let out of hell. At least, not yet.

"So," Cole stepped back and stared deeply into dark, accusing eyes, "does this mean that I'm too late?"

She shrugged again.

"Does this mean that everything we've shared up to this point was nothing more than a good time? That you can give it up with no more thought than this?"

"I believe that should be my line," Debbie drawled. "I'm the one who gave and gave with no promises, remember?"

He flushed angrily. He hated it when she was right. He also hated the rumbling of the crowd behind him. Unless he redeemed himself fast… He wondered if tarring and feathering was too outdated to worry about.

"I love you, Deborah Randall." Cole got down on one knee and tried to ignore the same woman in the crowd who was now sobbing openly. "Will you marry me?"

"I love you, too," she said, and raked her fingers through his hair, framing his face with her hands.

Relief blossomed until he realized that she'd never answered his question.

"Final boarding call for flight 1207 for Dallas—Ft. Worth and Oklahoma City," the attendant called.

Debbie turned around and started walking toward the gate.

Cole wanted to cry. What else could he say?

"You're leaving me anyway? You're going back to Oklahoma after all we've meant to each other? Why?" he begged. "Just tell me why."

Debbie couldn't prolong his agony any longer. She turned and smiled through her tears. "I'm going to get my mother's wedding dress," she said. "I'm not getting married without it."

Cole started to shake. "I ought to wring your little—"

She was in his arms.

"Last call for flight…"

"I've got to go," she said.

"I'm coming with you," Cole answered.

The small crowd of people who'd witnessed the entire altercation began to cheer and clap.

For the first time since the entire incident began, Debbie was at a loss for words.

"But you can't. You don't have a...they won't let you...."

"I'm a police officer," Cole said quietly. "Sometimes it pays to be special. I think I can talk them into letting me pay at the other end. Trust me?"

"Forever," Debbie said. And she did.

Epilogue

"We're going to be in trouble," Debbie warned as they pulled into the driveway.

Cole grinned. "It won't be the first time."

"They've probably been planning and planning. They're going to kill us."

"So don't tell them," Cole offered.

Debbie stared. "But think of the waste of time and money they'll go to if we don't."

"Think of the fun they'll miss if we do."

Debbie sighed. "We'll see," she said. "Just don't blurt it out too fast. Let's feel them out about the whole thing first."

Cole parked. He couldn't wipe the smile off his face. He'd been trying for the past two days. But it was still there, and he'd be damned if he'd worry about it again. And, if tonight was anything like last night, it might never come off.

The front door opened and his father and sister ran out.

"It's about time you two go home," Lily cried. "I thought you'd be here yesterday."

"Couldn't get a flight," Cole said calmly.

Debbie's stomach twisted. It wasn't *really* a lie. They couldn't get a flight because they hadn't tried.

Lily sighed and wrapped them both in a hug. "Wait till you see the flowers I've picked out."

Debbie sent Cole a piercing glare.

He shrugged and started loading his arms with bags. They'd packed everything possible and were shipping what hadn't fit.

"Need any help?" Morgan asked. Cole shifted several bags into his arms.

"What about me?" Case asked. Lily smiled at her husband, who sauntered outside as if he were on a weekend stroll. He was way too laid back for California time.

Cole loaded him, too. Finally they were ready to proceed. Debbie sent Cole one last look he couldn't misinterpret. They went into the house.

"So! Tell me everything," Lily said.

Debbie's eyebrows shot up into the fluff of her bangs and her face turned pink.

"Not on your life, Sis," Cole said softly.

Everyone laughed, except Debbie. She was starting to get a guilty conscience. She opened her mouth. Cole saw the look. He braced himself. It never came. Buddy sauntered into the room.

"You've got nerve," Debbie said, as she wrapped her arms around Buddy's neck and gave him a kiss. It was the first time she'd seen or spoken to him since her incident at the airport.

"I rather like to think of it as...initiative," Buddy claimed, and took the kiss as his reward for brilliance.

Cole grinned. "Your *initiative* almost got me shot, little brother."

"You look all right to me," Buddy remarked. And then he stared intently at them both before walking away. "In fact, if I didn't know better, I'd think you looked married."

Debbie nearly fainted. *Is he psychic too?*

For once Cole was speechless.

Everyone stared at them, waiting for them to deny it.

"Buddy!" Lily's shriek woke her baby. She sent Case a look that had him hastening to retrieve their son while she waited for her brother to reappear.

"You woke Charlie," he accused as he stuck his head around the corner.

"Why did you say that?" Lily asked.

Buddy rolled his eyes. Sometimes his family was too dense for words. "I said you woke him because I can hear him crying," he said distinctly. "Before he was quiet. Now he's not. Understand?"

"I think I'm going to kill you," Lily said shortly.

"Won't do any good," Morgan said. "I think he's

cloned himself in that damned room. If you hurt your brother, two more like him will come in his place."

Debbie wanted to hide. Cole slid his arm around her shoulders and pulled her gently against him. For better or worse, they were now in all this family mess together.

"I wasn't talking about my son's sleeping habits," Lily said shortly.

Buddy waited.

Lily wanted to strangle him. She'd forgotten how maddening he could be.

"I wanted to know what made you say what you did about Cole and Debbie."

"About what?"

Lily screamed. It was unlike her. She was a lady, always. She never lost her cool. Never. Unless Buddy was around.

"Why did you say Cole and Debbie looked married?"

"Oh that!" Buddy pointed. "I saw the rings. It's rather obvious, don't you think?"

Everyone gaped. For once, Buddy had them cold. He leaned against the wall and watched his family come to attention. They were a fascinating species.

"It's true." Lily was floored. "She's wearing rings."

"That doesn't necessarily mean—" Cole began.

"Cole, stop it," Debbie said softly. "No more."

He wrapped her in his arms. "You're right," he said. "No more. Not from any of you. Yes, we're married. Not because I wanted to leave any of you out of the ceremony, but because I'd waited long enough for Debbie to be part of this family. I nearly waited too long. I wasn't taking any more chances.''

''Makes sense to me,'' Case drawled as he walked back into the room carrying his son. ''Taking chances on women is deadly stuff. I can vouch for that.''

Lily smiled gently.

''If you want, we'll have another ceremony,'' Debbie offered. ''I brought my mother's wedding dress, just in case.''

''Far as I'm concerned, save it for your daughter's wedding,'' Case said. ''Getting married once is enough for any man. Twice is above and beyond. Besides, if I remember my own, you two should be about ready for the honeymoon. Where are you going?''

''We'll be gone until Wednesday,'' Cole said.

His brother-in-law grinned at the neat way he'd sidestepped the question. It was understandable.

''Where will you live when you come back?''

Lily's question took them all by surprise.

Morgan's face fell. He could hardly face the thought of Cole leaving. And Debbie had become another daughter. But it was only fair that they had their time alone.

Buddy lost his calm demeanor. He'd come to depend on Debbie greatly. He liked having someone fuss over him, and he definitely liked the way she cooked. What would he—?

"Who'll make me chocolate chip cookies?" Buddy asked aloud.

"I will, darling," Debbie said. She felt Cole's arms tighten around her. She could feel his approval. "And while we're gone, I expect you to keep your room clean."

Buddy nodded vigorously.

Cole laughed. *My God, but marriage to her is going to be one wild ride through life! I can't wait!*

"And, I don't want to come back and find out that there are no plates and glasses in the cupboards. Remember?"

"I remember," Buddy promised.

"Morgan—"

He jumped to attention. Obviously he wasn't going to escape the orders either. "If the twins come back while we're gone, explain the situation. And, I don't want to find out that you've quit your therapy."

Her warning was enough. He hugged her and smiled. "I promise, too, girl."

"How about me?" Cole whispered.

"Are you still here?" Debbie asked with practiced surprise. "Why aren't you packed? We've got a honeymoon to start."

"I don't need to pack," Cole drawled. "I sleep in the buff, remember?"

She blushed. It was just like him to tease her in front of the whole clan. "Yes, I remember it very well," she chided. "But what's that got to do with the trip?"

"Well, if we never get out of bed, what will I need with clothes?"

As usual, Debbie got the last word in...and the last laugh.

"After I'm through with you," she drawled, "they'll have to bury you in something. Pack your good suit. You'll want to look nice for the funeral."

Cole looked stunned. And then he laughed.

"It won't take long," he said. "I've only got one suit."

* * * * *

In celebration of our 20th anniversary,
Silhouette Books proudly presents
the first three Silhouette Desire novels
by bestselling author

ANNETTE BROADRICK

in a landmark 3-in-1 collection!

Three magnetic men, brimming with sex
appeal, have held a tight rein on their volcanic
desires—until now. For they are born to claim,
cherish and protect the women fated
to be theirs.

Maximum Marriage:
Men on a Mission
(on sale 10/00)

Then, in November, watch for
MARRIAGE PREY
in Silhouette Desire.
This unforgettable love story is a brand-new sequel to
MAXIMUM MARRIAGE: MEN ON A MISSION.

Available at your favorite retail outlet.

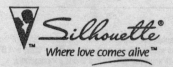

Silhouette®

Where love comes alive™

Visit Silhouette at www.eHarlequin.com   PSMAX

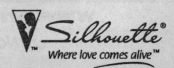

Silhouette invites you to come back to Whitehorn, Montana...

MONTANA MAVERICKS

WED IN WHITEHORN—
12 BRAND-NEW stories that capture living and loving beneath the Big Sky where legends live on and love lasts forever!

MM

June 2000—
Lisa Jackson *Lone Stallion's Lady* (#1)

July 2000—
Laurie Paige *Cheyenne Bride* (#2)

August 2000—
Jennifer Greene *You Belong to Me* (#3)

September 2000—
Victoria Pade *The Marriage Bargain* (#4)

And the adventure continues...

Available at your favorite retail outlet.

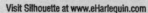